Knight Prisoner

by Margaret Hodges

ONE LITTLE DRUM
WHAT'S FOR LUNCH, CHARLEY?
A CLUB AGAINST KEATS
TELL IT AGAIN:
GREAT TALES FROM AROUND THE WORLD (*editor*)
THE SECRET IN THE WOODS
THE WAVE
THE HATCHING OF JOSHUA COBB
CONSTELLATION (*editor*)
SING OUT, CHARLEY!
LADY QUEEN ANNE
THE MAKING OF JOSHUA COBB
THE GORGON'S HEAD
PERSEPHONE AND THE SPRINGTIME
THE FIRE BRINGER
BALDUR AND THE MISTLETOE
HOPKINS OF THE MAYFLOWER
THE FREEWHEELING OF JOSHUA COBB
KNIGHT PRISONER

KNIGHT PRISONER

*The Tale of Sir Thomas Malory
and His King Arthur*

MARGARET HODGES

Decorations by Don Bolognese and Elaine Raphael

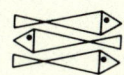

Farrar, Straus and Giroux
NEW YORK

Copyright © 1976 by Margaret Hodges
All rights reserved

FIRST PRINTING, 1976

Printed in the United States of America
Published simultaneously in Canada
by McGraw Hill Ryerson Ltd., Toronto
Designed by Herb Johnson

Library of Congress Cataloging in Publication Data

Hodges, Margaret.
   Knight prisoner.

   Bibliography: p.
   Includes index.
   1. Malory, Thomas, Sir, 15th cent.—Juvenile literature. 2. Authors, English—Middle English, 1100–1500—Biography—Juvenile literature. [1. Malory, Thomas, Sir, 15th cent. 2. Authors, English] I. Title.
PR2045.H6   823'.2 [B] [92]   76-26693
ISBN 0-374-34269-5

To Stith Thompson

AMERICAN GENTLEMAN,

SCHOLAR AND FOLKLORIST,

DESCENDANT OF THE BEAUCHAMP FAMILY

Contents

FOREWORD ix

ONE   GARETH   3
TWO   LAUNCELOT   19
THREE   ARTHUR   37
FOUR   GUINEVERE   69
FIVE   GALAHAD   101
SIX   MORDRED   125
SEVEN   MALORY   163

AFTERWORD   173
ACKNOWLEDGMENTS   181
BIBLIOGRAPHY   185
INDEX   191

Foreword

SIR THOMAS MALORY of Warwickshire was one of the glorious company of those who have written in prison—St. Paul, Columbus, Cervantes, John Bunyan, Sir Thomas More, Sir Walter Raleigh—the list could go on and on into our own day. Thomas Malory's work, the translating and retelling of Arthurian legends into the English of his day, became the *Morte Darthur*, which William Caxton published in 1485, fourteen years after Malory's death. C. S. Lewis has said of the *Morte Darthur* that "it alone of all medieval prose romances has survived as a living book into our own century."

We know very little about Thomas Malory, but he was born about the beginning of the fifteenth century and most scholars believe that he came of a good family who owned

Foreword

property called Newbold Revel in the parish of Monks Kirby near Coventry in Warwickshire. During his lifetime he served several lords, the first being Richard Beauchamp, Earl of Warwick, who was known in his day as "the Father of Courtesy." Thomas Malory fought under the banner of Henry V in France during the last years of the Hundred Years' War, and it is believed that he was at Rouen when Joan of Arc was burned at the stake.

After his return from France he served as a Member of Parliament for Warwickshire and later for towns in Wiltshire and Dorset. At about the same time he fell afoul of the law and was accused of numerous crimes, including theft, plundering, and rape. The Wars of the Roses were breaking out and Thomas Malory as a Lancastrian may have been the victim of Yorkist political enemies. Or he may have been guilty, as charged. He pleaded "not guilty," but he was put in prison and kept there for most of his remaining years, until his death in London on March 14, 1471. He was buried in Greyfriars Abbey, from which he had borrowed some books about King Arthur and his knights. He may have died in prison. We do not know.

The coming years may throw new light into the shadows of Newgate, Malory's last prison. We also want to know where Malory's manuscript was kept after his death, until Caxton printed it. Perhaps Malory's grandson, Nicholas, had it. Perhaps the monks of Greyfriars Abbey kept it in their great library.

In 1934 a manuscript was found by Walter Oakeshott, a librarian at Winchester, the town which Malory had called Camelot. This Winchester manuscript was older than Caxton's, though it was evidently not the one which Malory himself had penned. It comprised a series of Arthurian

Foreword

tales, one of which ended with a colophon, or note addressed to the reader:

> Here endeth this tale, as the French book saith, from the marriage of king Uther unto [the time of] king Arthur that reigned after him and did many battles.
>
> And this book endeth whereas sir Launcelot and sir Tristram come to court. Who that will make any more let him seek other books of king Arthur or of sir Launcelot or sir Tristram; for this was drawn by a knight prisoner, sir Thomas Malory [Malleorre], that God send him good recover. Amen. Explicit.

Oakeshott said of his discovery: "The colophon, with its spelling of Malory's name, and its 'prisoner,' is like a voice from the great deeps. One makes so many absurd guesses in this game of scholarship that it is reassuring to have one's theories substantiated by documentary evidence."

Forty years later we still have to make "many absurd guesses" about Thomas Malory. This book cannot be a full and factual biography; it is, rather, "The Tale of Sir Thomas Malory." The known facts are here—the births and reigns and deaths of kings and queens, the places and dates of battles. But who are the heroes and who are the villains? That depends on the point of view. Now and then we think we see Malory's point of view in the pages of the *Morte Darthur*, but we are guessing.

The response to the discovery of the Winchester manuscript is still growing. It seems that scholars cannot rest until they have fully solved the mysteries relating to Malory's life. Behind this impulse is a sense of obligation to the "knight prisoner" who made us see what the old tales of Arthur and his knights really mean, who made us see how we long to believe in a golden age that has been and can be again.

Knight Prisoner

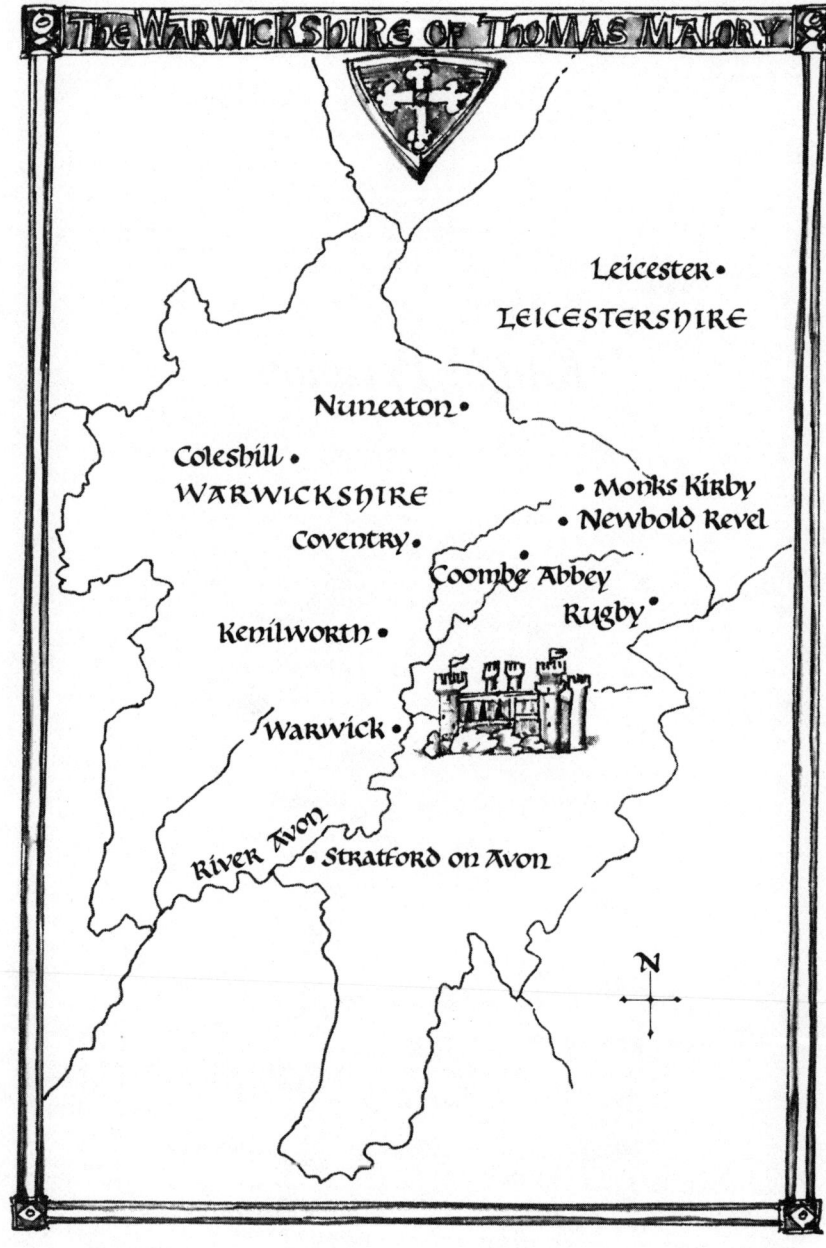

GARETH

> "*Sir, said Beaumains, I would fain be of good fame and of good knighthood . . . I came of good men, for I dare say my father was a noble man . . .*"
>
> **THE TALE OF SIR GARETH OF ORKNEY**

THE old man, Thomas Malory, turned on his side and opened his eyes to look toward the window of his cell. It let in only hubbub and stench from the London Shambles; no light yet. He looked for Arcturus. Whenever he woke in the dark he looked for Arcturus, usually in vain, as now. But it was somewhere in the heavens and in due course he would find it again with the constellation of the Great Bear. To Thomas Malory that constellation meant Warwick and Richard Beauchamp. Arcturus was the star that meant Arthur the King. He too would appear again. It had been promised.

Once as a boy Thomas had fallen asleep astride his horse somewhere near Warwick Castle, and had not wakened until it was full dark. Hopelessly lost, he splashed through marshes, urged his weary mount up hill and down dale, and took the lash of black branches on his face and shoulders, until suddenly the night sky cleared and he saw Arcturus and the Great Bear and knew how to go toward home.

The memory of it now, sixty years later, still gave him a sense of security. His old battle wounds ached but nothing could take away the fact that he had once been young and straight and strong, able to sleep anywhere, even in the saddle. A stone floor would do, or a battlefield with his shield for a pillow, or the wave-swept deck of a ship on a Channel crossing. Thomas Malory had slept on all of them in his time, and could do it again, if need be. He had slept in other prisons, too, and survived them all. He would survive this one. But it was too early to allow himself to wake. Carefully he arranged his knees so that they were covered by the blanket. In Newgate Prison, blankets came dear, and his purse was lean. Thank God, he had learned from youth to sleep wherever fortune chose to put him for the night.

From St. Paul's steeple the bells rang the half hour, and a moment later the bells of St. Bartholomew's, then the chimes of St. Nicholas. He would soon hear the brothers singing matins from the chapel of Greyfriars Abbey. Before long the brother would be coming from Greyfriars library with the French books and the old poems which Thomas Malory needed for his work. Sir Richard Whittington had given the money to found that library and it had grown to be one of London's great treasures.

While he waited in the cold and the dark, he half slept again and thought that he had wakened at Newbold Revel in his own chamber, where he had slept as a boy. He dreamed that it was Whitsuntide; bright sunlight streamed in through the open window. Rushes, fresh-cut in spring fields and strewn on the floor, made a sweetness around him. His cousin Philip Chetwynd, who had come for a visit, was in the bed with him, singing softly to himself the old round:

> *Summer is a-coming in,*
> *Loud sing cuckoo!*
> *Groweth seed, and bloweth mead,*
> *And springs the wood anew . . .*

Thomas joined in at the proper place:

> *Summer is a-coming in,*
> *Loud sing cuckoo!*

Then they fell to putting English words as well as they could to a Welsh ballad about King Arthur. It had been sung last night by Sir John Malory's minstrel, who was taken prisoner when the King put down a rebellion in Wales. Sir John said that the minstrel was not much of a prize, since no one would offer a ransom for him. He sang the same song over and over. At first he could hardly be understood, except when he happened to come to the name of Arthur and another name that might be Merlin the enchanter.

Later, Thomas learned it all by heart, this "Death Song of the British Kings" of time long gone, with its marvelous pictures of the hero Owein, whose "keen-edged spears were like the wings of the dawn." And there were glimpses of a last terrible battle and all the gallant knights and the kings dead on the bloody field. "The host of broad England sleeps with the light in their eyes . . ."

While the boys were still singing, they heard horses' hooves in the stone courtyard and rushed for the window. Sir John, Thomas's father, was below, mounting to ride. He wore his fine surcoat embroidered all over with "the ragged staff" that marked him as a liege man of the Earl of Warwick. His hawk was not on his wrist, nor his hounds behind him. Only two bowmen and his hostler, a bandy-legged fellow, rode after him through the gateway, over the moat, past the windmill, and out of sight. Like any right-minded Warwickshire boy, Thomas would have given his soul for a morning of hunting with his father on such a day as this, in clear weather and bright, with the birds singing from every bough and every tree in full leaf. But his father was evidently bent on official business of some sort. This day Thomas was doomed to go to school as usual.

He doused his head in a basin of cold water, packed a pouch with bread and cheese from the pantry, and ran into the solar, where his mother already sat by the oriel window, combing her hair in the morning sun. He knelt at her feet for a hasty blessing and then made for the stable, Philip close behind him. Philip had a horse of his own and pulled Thomas up after him.

It was a two-mile journey to school at Monks Kirby. There in the chamber over the church porch Thomas would pass a long dull day while Philip, with no one to say him nay, rode on westward to have a look at the noble walls of Coombe Abbey and perhaps to see what adventures he could find at this Whitsuntide in Coventry, eight miles away. At the very least, there would be a grand procession, a pageant, or a miracle play, with God and the Devil on stage fighting for a man's soul.

At Monks Kirby, Thomas slid down from Philip's horse

and slowly climbed the stone stairs to the schoolroom in the tower of St. Edith's church. He did not know that it would be his last day in that school.

An aged brother from Kirby Priory taught such pupils as came. He was French, one of two monks remaining with the prior in the tumbledown buildings which had once housed seven Carthusians from Anjou. The youngest and most devout of the brothers had recently been transferred to a new and flourishing Carthusian monastery, a good administrative decision, no doubt, but high-handed. The ailing prior and the two homesick lay brothers stayed on at Kirby Priory, observing only whatever parts of the Carthusian rule suited their failing strength, dim eyes, and arthritic bones. The tithes collected by Sir John Malory's bailiff were still sent to the priory, but Sir John grudged them. He got little enough in return, at best a few prayers and a bit of schooling for his son.

However, even a little schooling was important for a boy like Thomas, whose father was poor and proud. Education opened doors that would otherwise be closed in his face, so Thomas paid attention at school. He learned his Latin grammar by heart, repeating it after Brother Guillaume. The old man taught from a tattered Donatus, the only book remaining from a dozen volumes that had once been the glory of the priory. Few schools had so many books. But with the Donatus alone, much could be learned.

Eight boys of the neighborhood came to the school, two little ones timidly gabbling their ABC's, their Paternoster, Ave, and Creed, or counting to ten on their fingers. The older boys had slates on which they traced their grammar lessons from copies of the Donatus made by Brother Guillaume. When they finished the Donatus he would have taken them as far as he could go; they would at least be launched for an attack on the higher learning in all its forms.

Every word spoken at school was in Latin, but on sunny days Brother Guillaume came with the boys to eat his bread and cheese in the churchyard, where he allowed himself to speak his own tongue. He sat warming his back against a tombstone and telling stories in the French of Anjou, where the language was purest, or so he said. He implied that it was far superior to the Norman French spoken by his pupils.

Some of his stories were about a knight named Gaheret, who was very tall and strong and large-handed. Brother Guillaume would stretch out his own thin hand to explain the meaning, "large-handed" or "generous." Other stories were about Tristan, the greatest of all hunters, who, like Thomas's father, could tell all the fine points in the arts of hunting and blowing the hunting horn. Still others were of Launcelot, the bravest and most courteous of knights, he who crossed a sword-bridge, grievously wounded thereby, to reach his lady love, Guenièvre.

Thomas liked these stories. He thought of himself as Gaheret and of his father as Tristan the hunter. Thomas had never met a knight to compare with Launcelot, but Warwickshire had a Launcelot, the Earl of Warwick himself, now on pilgrimage to the Holy Land. All England knew Richard Beauchamp, Earl of Warwick, as the very flower of knighthood. Thomas imagined him as the knight in the wall painting at the end of the great hall at Newbold Revel, kneeling in all-night vigil before an altar on which his Sword lay.

Thomas knew the meaning of the Sword. All those who

wished to be knights learned the meaning. The blade was Faith, which must be kept shining bright. The scabbard was Purity and meant that the body should be kept clean, as the scabbard must be clean in order to be worthy of the blade it covered. The Sword as a whole meant Power, kept in control and used only in the service of God and man. At the knight's side stood a lady holding a Cup in both hands. The Cup was that from which Our Lord drank at the Last Supper, and its meaning was too high and holy for any man to understand while he was alive. Above these figures were painted a royal dragon and a bear, the bear that meant Arthur and the earls of Warwick.

At Newbold Revel the Welsh minstrel sang ballads about this Cup, the Holy Grail, and other stories very like Brother Guillaume's except that the names were slightly different and the places seemed to be Wales or Cornwall or Ireland. One day Thomas eagerly asked Brother Guillaume where the stories had taken place and whether they were true. Brother Guillaume said that all were true and had happened in Anjou or elsewhere in France during the memory of some who were still living. No one dreamed of contradicting the schoolmaster, but it was puzzling.

Another puzzle was the question of Anjou itself. Sir John had said that Anjou belonged to King Henry IV of England. When Thomas repeated this information to Brother Guillaume, the old man's face turned dark and sour. He muttered to himself, and soon afterward, for no reason, gave Thomas a blow on the ear.

That evening Thomas did not speak of the blow, for when he was punished at school, he was generally punished again at home if his father heard of it. Instead he simply asked his father to explain the matter of Anjou. Sir

John's answer covered more than three hundred years and was so long-winded and complex that Thomas very nearly fell asleep over it.

It seemed that William of Normandy, he who was known as "the Conqueror," had been promised the throne of England and had come across the Channel from France in 1066 to take what was rightfully his. According to Sir John, Thomas had an ancestor, a noble Norman who had come with the Conqueror and had fought bravely against Harold the Saxon at Battle Abbey near Hastings. William had rewarded his Norman knights with lands and with Saxon serfs, as was only just and right. After those days there had been a confusion of English kings; Williams, Richards, Edwards, and Henrys had come and gone. Some had been forced to fight for lands in France that rightfully belonged to them by descent from the first William and through marriages of English kings to French princesses.

Within the memory of living men, English soldiers fighting for King Edward III had won great victories against the French, once at Crécy and again at Poitiers, so that Edward had been called King of France as well as King of England. *There* had been a true king! But the French had broken their treaty and denied him his rights. You could never trust the French.

Of the present King, the fourth Henry, Sir John had not much to say. Some declared him to be the rightful heir to the English throne, others called him a usurper. Plots, counterplots, and rebellions had filled his reign, the French helping the Welsh and the Scots against him. Now the King was said to have leprosy, or something more shameful. Whatever his disease, he was broken in body and mind.

Nor could much be expected from the young Prince of Wales. He would inherit the throne on the death of the King, which must come soon. Prince Hal had been born and trained for kingship, and had been a bachelor knight since the age of twelve, bold and strong and handsome, a fine athlete and a fearless warrior. But he was wild and dissolute, likely to follow in the footsteps of his sinful father. England had fallen on evil days and worse, no doubt, lay ahead.

Sir John then told both boys, Thomas and Philip, a piece of news that was to change their lives. Acting on information that the Earl of Warwick would soon be home from his pilgrimage, he had ridden that day to Warwick Castle to arrange that they should enter the noble household as pages. Philip's father had sent him to Newbold Revel for this very purpose, but lest the boys hope for too much, nothing had been said of the plan until it was a certainty.

Because Philip's family was well-to-do, he was sure to make an excellent impression on arrival with his own horse and with his tunic and hose of fine soft wool, his shoes of the best leather. Thomas had no such advantages. He must make do with what he had and hold his head high. He would have no horse at first, but Sir John would procure one for him somehow by the time he became a squire. When a villein died, his best animal would go to Sir John as lord of the manor. The bailiff had told him of a good horse which he would soon have from a tenant whose aged father was inconveniently lingering on past his expected threescore years and ten.

Sometimes, while Thomas was at his lessons in the tower room of St. Edith's, his father was holding a manorial court in the nave of the church. There tithes were paid, disputes were settled, and inquests were held. It was Sir John's custom to open the court and glare with grim brow while a handful of huddled peasants bobbed, pulled off caps, and tugged forelocks. Then, as often as possible, Sir John would stalk away, leaving his bailiff to collect rents or assess fines for work undone. Sir John did not want to hear about other men's troubles; he did not want to see men on their knees, weeping. He had his own payments to make at Warwick Castle, just as the Earl of Warwick made his to the King. From the highest to the lowest, all must pay.

The King himself could not always meet the cost of the wars against the Welsh, the Scots, and the French. Because of the wars Newbold Revel now needed repairs which Sir John could not afford, and even the great towers of Warwick Castle had begun to crumble in the days of Crécy and Poitiers. To make matters worse, since the Black Death many cottages stood empty and many fields lay fallow. Those that were left had to yield more.

It took a sharp-eyed bailiff at Newbold Revel to know the proper yield of crops and to keep account of flocks and herds. To be a bailiff was no enviable task, for the peasants hated him and they could be crafty and dangerous. Give them an inch and they would take an ell. Everyone remembered the mad priest, John Ball, who had gone about Kent in the days of King Richard II rousing passions in the villeins with his talk of a day when everything would be held in common and there would be no villeins and no gentlemen. "We be all come from one father and one mother, Adam and Eve," John Ball had said. "The lords are clothed in velvet and stuffs trimmed with fur, but we in poor cloth. They have their wines, spices, and good bread: and we have bread made from chaff and only water to drink . . .

We be called their bondsmen, we be beaten. Let us go to the King, he is young, and show him what slavery we be in." These were wild words.

Not long afterward, another Kentish fellow named Wat Tyler—they were all rebels down there—had smashed the skull of a tax collector who had ravished Tyler's daughter. Serfs followed Wat Tyler all the way to London, looting, burning, and even murdering the Archbishop of Canterbury. The end of it was that the Lord Mayor stabbed Wat Tyler, and John Ball was hanged, drawn, and quartered. The four pieces of his body were sent around from village to village as a warning. The young King Richard spoke the final words of the drama: "Serfs ye are, and serfs ye shall remain."

So it must be. From the king down through his barons, bishops, and abbots, and below them to lords of the manor and those who labored on the land, whether freemen, yeomen, humble villeins, or serfs without possessions of any kind, all must keep their place, and all must pay to maintain the order of things. In this order Sir John Malory had his own place to maintain, not without difficulty, and he had his son, Thomas, whose place must be assured. As a first step, the bailiff would get him a horse.

His father and mother had already begun his training in courtesy as a rule of life, for much more than book learning was required of a boy who would become a squire and then a knight. Thomas learned to blow the hunting horn with clear round notes, to sit his horse well, and to hunt skillfully. He trained and carried a hawk according to the complex rules of the ancient sport of falconry. Later would come the use of the lance, the even deadlier hand gisarme, the long sword, the short sword, the dagger, and the mace.

When he became the squire to some noble knight, Thomas would master the art of serving gracefully at table. When he himself ate, he would not stuff his mouth full or eat noisily. He must not spit out food. And he should refrain from scratching the backs of any dogs that might be under the table.

In the household of the Earl of Warwick there were servants whose whole duty was to entertain with music and dance, with ballad singing and storytelling; but Thomas, as the son of a gentleman, should be able to pick up a lute or recorder and play some little air if asked to do so. Already his mother had taught him a favorite for Christmastide:

> *I sing of a maiden*
> *That is matchless:*
> *The king of all kings*
> *For her son she chose.*
>
> *He came as still*
> *Where his mother was,*
> *As dew in April*
> *That falleth on the grass* . . .

In his pre-dawn revery, Thomas Malory, knight prisoner of Newgate, saw his father and mother as they had been on the long-ago night when he first learned that he was to leave them—his father seated at the table in the great hall at Newbold Revel, eating his supper and explaining matters to Thomas. He had always thought his father a handsome man, though the styles of those old days seemed odd as he looked back on them: the hair cut straight around the head above the ears, the robe worn for comfort at home, full and long, with sleeves reaching in points to the ground.

His mother had been an heiress of the Revell family,

from which the manor took its name. He had always thought her beautiful in her soft woolen gown, her high headdress and floating veil, all too simple for today's rich tastes. On that last night she held a handful of parchment leaves written over with verses for him to repeat:

> *Be courteous to God, and kneel down*
> *On both knees with great devotion . . .*

But to any man, even to his lord or his king, he should bend only one knee. And he must shun

> *The devil, the flesh, the world also,*
> *That work for mankind so much woe.*

He had said all the words after her while the light faded and the great hall filled with shadows until he could no longer see the painted knight with his Sword and the painted lady with her Cup.

He woke again at Newgate when the brothers of Greyfriars began to sing their matins. The lay brother would soon be coming to the prison, bringing prayers and other comforts. For Thomas Malory he also brought pens, ink, paper, and the books from the abbey library. He brought the French books one at a time, for they were rare and valuable. They told the same stories that the minstrels had sung in Sir Thomas's boyhood, the same stories that Brother Guillaume had told in the churchyard at Monks Kirby.

But today he would not need to consult the books. Today he would work on a story that was taking shape in his own mind, a tale of Gareth of Orkney—Gaheret, as Brother Guillaume had called him—who came to King Arthur's court, young, unknown, poor, and proud, as he, Thomas

Malory, had been on the day long ago when he arrived with Philip Chetwynd at Warwick Castle and first presented himself to Richard Beauchamp.

With an effort of will he put out of his mind all that had come afterward: the holy Cup dishonored; the Sword drenched in blood, not in the service of God or man, but for greed and blood lust; the women violated and ravished; and that one strange Maid who had been burned at the stake in Rouen; the war lost; the kings and lords not worth serving. He would not think of these things.

Today he would write of how Gareth came to the King's court mounted and armed but poorly, and accompanied by a dwarf, though he himself amazed the whole court because of his great height and strength. How he asked only for food and lodging, so that Sir Kay despised him and made fun of his big hands and sent him to feed in the kitchen, little knowing that Gareth was King Arthur's own nephew. How he learned the arts and skills of chivalry, beat Sir Kay soundly, and was knighted by Sir Launcelot, whom he most admired. How he went with the proud Lady Lyonet to release her sister Lady Lyonesse, who was besieged by an evil knight. How the Lady Lyonet gave him nothing but hard words all along the way, saying that he smelled of the kitchen and stood tall only as a common weed stands tall above the good corn. How he overcame every enemy in his path until the Lady Lyonet begged his pardon and the Lady Lyonesse said to King Arthur, "I would rather have Sir Gareth for my husband than any king or prince, and if I may not have him I will have none. For, my lord Arthur, he is my first love and he shall be my last, and if you will suffer him to have his free will and choice, I daresay he will have me."

Time sped and Thomas Malory was in good spirits while he worked on his story. It came easily, set like a hundred tales that the minstrels told, and yet his own story, unfolding in the springtime of his life. It was his own story with the dark side forgotten, and it ended as all tales should, with lovers wedded, and with great riches given them, "that royally they might live till their lives end."

Then Thomas Malory wrote, AND I PRAY YOU ALL THAT READ THIS TALE TO PRAY FOR HIM THAT WROTE THIS, THAT GOD SEND HIM GOOD DELIVERANCE SOON AND HASTILY. AMEN. HERE ENDS THE TALE OF SIR GARETH OF ORKNEY.

LAUNCELOT

> "Then, sir, this is that other gift that you shall grant me: that Sir Launcelot shall make me knight."
>
> **THE TALE OF SIR GARETH OF ORKNEY**

In the darkest days of his imprisonment Thomas Malory knew that he had not long to live and raged at the thought of his death. Why should he be old and ill, numbering his days, when other men in the street below his window, greedy merchants, sniveling shoemakers, greasy hog stickers, walked free in the open air with years of youth and health ahead of them? Why should his own time be running out? And where had the brave days gone with their brave dreams, the days when a man could find a good lord and serve him with faith and honor? He would remember his own good lord to the last day of his life.

When Thomas Malory had come to Warwick Castle as a page, Richard Beauchamp, Earl of Warwick, was already known as the best knight of the world. He was twenty-three years old, freshly returned from two years as a knight errant and pilgrim to the Holy Land, and he had every grace that the code of courtesy and chivalry could bestow upon a man of noble lineage.

Richard Beauchamp traced his family line back to King Gwidard, who, according to the records, "died about the same year that our Lord died," and he also claimed descent from King Constantine, grandfather to King Arthur, the mighty warrior. Another ancestor was King Gwayr, cousin of King Arthur, and a giant killer. This giant had torn a great tree from the earth and ripped away the branches to make a club. Gwayr overcame him, and the club, "the ragged staff" on the Warwick coat of arms, was a symbol of his victory. An Earl of Warwick, called in the ancient records Arthgal or Arthal, had been a knight of King Arthur's Round Table, "a lord of royal blood, and witty in all his deeds." The name might be written Arthe or Narthe, "as much as to say in Welsh, a bear." From earliest times the bear was carved over the gateway of the town of Warwick. One could not think of the Warwicks without thinking of the bear and of King Arthur.

On the death of his father, Richard Beauchamp had inherited the enormous Warwick bed, covered and hung with silk all embroidered with the sign of the bear. It was there to inspire his first thoughts in the morning and his dreams at night. At dinner in the great hall of Warwick Castle he faced a tapestry nine yards long and three yards high, depicting the coronation of King Arthur. It had been made in Flanders, where Arthur was famous, as he was in all the known world. The tapestry loomed above Warwick knights, squires, and pages, down to the youngest at the table in the far corner of the hall where Thomas Malory sat. To be there was to live again in the days of King Arthur.

Launcelot

Thomas first saw Richard Beauchamp in the tiltyard, where he and Philip Chetwynd had been sent to watch the older boys at practice. The beginners were mounted on small horses and were pitted against each other in pairs, armed with blunt lances. The bigger and more expert, almost men, were riding by turn in a circle, aiming their lances at a metal ring as they galloped past it. On the word of command from an elder knight, their teacher and trainer, they leaped from their horses and again vaulted into the saddle. Thomas was all eyes. His heart hammered at the thought that he was to live this life and learn these skills.

Then he saw a tall man coming from the gardens beyond the tiltyard. Richard Beauchamp wore a long robe belted with gold. A heavy gold collar circled his neck. His hair was light, his fair skin tanned by his long travels. As he came near at a measured pace, neither fast nor slow, Thomas saw the slender oval face that meant Norman blood. Only courtesy marked this high-born face. The grins, frowns, grimaces that lined other men's cheeks and brows had left no trace here. The expression was mild, impassive, pleasant, calm as the sea on a summer day, but, like the sea, awesome with its look of power held in reserve. At his side, her hand on his arm, walked a young lady, and behind them came a dozen gentlemen. Thomas saw the ragged staff worked in silver on their rich surcoats.

The news of the Earl's presence rippled over the yard and the contesting squires doubled their efforts to excel under the eye of their lord. For some time he watched with evident approval. Then, to the wonder and delight of the pages, he crossed with his lady to where they stood.

Conscious that the lady smelled deliciously of flowers

2 1

and spices, they dropped to their knees, not daring to raise their eyes. As the Earl asked their names, they answered one by one in voices shrill or trembling between fear and pleasure. Thomas could not make a sound, but when the Earl with a kind smile had gone on his way, he vowed that one day the great man, his good lord from this day on, would know the name of Thomas Malory.

That night, as was usual, a hundred retainers, knights, squires, and pages gathered to dine in the great hall. Torches flung their light on the King Arthur tapestry and higher against the shadowy ceiling, its beams carved with so many angels that all the space above seemed filled with rushing wings. Minstrels played and sang in the music gallery, while the Earl and his lady sat at a dais, dining on roasted swan and peacock from their own preserves, on sweet figs and raisins and wine from Spain.

In a far corner with the other pages Thomas Malory and Philip Chetwynd dined more simply on meat pies and ale, as was fitting for boys. The servants, despising Thomas's plain tunic and cloak, served him last and least. He swore inwardly that he would find ways to prove his brawn and brain to the servants as well as to his lord.

After dinner the Earl again singled out the pages for special notice, calling them to sit on the lower step of the dais. Then he signaled to a favorite minstrel, who took a place near the hearth and on his lute struck the first notes of "Guy of Warwick." Every boy knew the story, but now they heard it sung in the very castle where the old tale had begun and ended, and sung for Richard Beauchamp, the reincarnation of Guy himself.

The story told how Guy of Warwick in ancient days had fought and killed all adversaries and had won in marriage the hand of a beautiful lady, Felice, a name meaning "happiness." He left her to go on pilgrimage to the Holy Land, where he slew a thousand Saracens. He defended the helpless against a dragon and against a giant who was armed with a cartload of Danish battle-axes, great clubs with iron knobs, steel lances, and iron hooks. Guy, in disguise, still dressed as a holy palmer, fought with only the sign of the cross to protect him. At a thrilling point in the tale, the giant cut off the head of Guy's horse, but Guy leaped to his feet and fought on until evening, when he at last cut off the giant's head.

The ladies loved best to hear how Guy, traveling through Normandy, came upon a fair damsel condemned to be burned at the stake on a false charge, unless she could find a champion to undergo ordeal by battle for her. They clapped their hands when Guy arrived in the very nick of time, fought all of the maiden's accusers, defeated them, and saved her.

But the end of the story made the ladies weep and the boys yawn, for although Guy returned from his pilgrimage, he did not return to the arms of his Felice. Instead, he concealed himself two miles from Warwick Castle at a place still known as Guy's Cliff. There in a cave he fasted and prayed, repenting of having spilled so much blood. Sometimes he went to the castle and begged for alms, but never made himself known to his faithful wife until the last day of his life, when he sent her his ring and she came to him in his hermitage. Among shady woods, crystal streams, and flowering meadows—the minstrel's voice lingered over each pure sad note—Guy kissed her and died.

In the hush that followed the story, Richard Beauchamp pointed to the sword of Guy of Warwick, which hung on the wall, and told the boys to be worthy of it. He told how even in Jerusalem the Sultan's lieutenant knew the tale of Guy and, when he had heard of the Earl's presence there, had feasted him and given him three precious stones, gifts of silk, and gold for his servants. All this was done to honor the descendant of the famous Sir Guy of Warwick.

On many nights after his arrival at Warwick as a page, Thomas Malory heard more of the Earl's "wander years," which had matched so well the example of Guy. He had seen many holy relics, but had quested in vain for the Holy Grail. No one could tell him exactly how the Grail would look if it could be found, and perhaps no knight now living had a heart pure enough for that high privilege. He, Richard Beauchamp, a sinful man, would never find it; of that he was sure. But everywhere in European books and manuscripts, in wall paintings and in the sculpture of cathedrals and castles, the Holy Grail was pictured. Often it seemed to be a Cup surrounded by light and fragrance, perhaps the very Cup from which Christ drank at the Last Supper. In Germany, Richard Beauchamp had found a book telling the story of Sir Parsival, a knight of King Arthur's Round Table, who had indeed seen the Grail. The Earl had bought the book for a high price, wrapped it in linen, and brought it home as a treasure for the library of Warwick Castle.

It is written in Holy Scripture that there is "a time of peace." In time of peace Richard Beauchamp was a gentle scholar, a poet, and a devoted husband. His first wife, a daughter of the illustrious de Lisle family, was the child bride whom Thomas Malory remembered meeting on his arrival at Warwick Castle. She had been still young when she died. The second wife was the Countess Isabella, to whom Richard Beauchamp wrote charming love songs.

> *Her flowering youth in lustiness*
> *Grounded in virtuous humbleness*
> *I you assure...*
> *And I her man both whole and true*
> *Have been, and changed for no one new*
> *Nor ever will my heart remove*
> *From her service...*

Writing verses for ladies was only one of the minor graces of knightly courtesy in a time of peace. The major principles were more weighty, and Richard Beauchamp was devoted to all of them. It was no empty form when as a candidate for the noble order of knighthood he fasted, bathed, and clothed himself in white for a night-long vigil kneeling before an altar on which his sword was laid. There he prayed and meditated on his oath: to love God and mankind and high deeds, to defend with his life the honor and chastity of women, to be loyal to the king, to live a pure and stainless life, to fight for the right against might, to protect the poor and distressed, and to use strength and power only in the service of others, especially those who were oppressed and too weak to help themselves. All of these things the knights of the Round Table had sworn, and after their example, every knight since the days of King Arthur.

Holy Scripture also says: "There is a time of war." Often, of course, the Earl's sword had been red with blood. Even his wander years had not been spent entirely in prayer and pilgrimage. As a knight errant, wherever he met a noble challenger, he took up the gauntlet, jousting, fighting with axes, swords, and daggers, soundly defeating his opponent in every combat, but usually sparing his life with a gallant gesture. In the tournament or in battle Thomas Malory had seen the Earl's face contorted with rage, teeth clenched, eyes blazing. This was no sin. Battle rage had made it possible for heroes of old to conquer giants and dragons. And in the days of King Henry V, when Richard Beauchamp had fought with battle rage, the King's cause was just, was it not? By battle and siege, men, women, and children died; but if the King's cause was just, their deaths were not upon the heads of the King's captains.

Richard Beauchamp had called himself a sinner, unworthy to see the Holy Grail, yet in the whole course of his life, Thomas Malory saw no sin. In all the tales that he had read, in all that he had heard told or sung, one knight alone compared with his memories of his good lord, Richard Beauchamp, Earl of Warwick. Only Launcelot could stand beside him. The tales of Launcelot were written in French in the book that came to Thomas Malory from the library in Greyfriars Abbey. But when his work was finished, and he must live to finish it, he would have made these stories into plain English, so that all Englishmen, if they could read, might know Launcelot, and, reading of him, think of Richard Beauchamp, who had been like Launcelot "the best knight of the world." Surely they would see the likeness.

Not long after his return from the Holy Land, the Earl was gone again. He was often at court, or in Scotland or Wales. Then King Henry IV appointed him deputy Captain of Calais, replacing his own son, Prince Hal. It was a post of great honor and responsibility, for Calais, separated from England by narrow straits, was the key that opened the door to commerce with France.

Launcelot

The young pages at Warwick learned how King Edward III in the glorious year of 1347 had taken the town from the French. During that whole year the stubborn burghers behind Calais's strong walls had starved to death, until at last six of the richest and most respected citizens submitted to Edward's will and came out of the gates barefooted and with ropes around their necks, delivering the keys of Calais into the hands of an English executioner. Then King Edward's queen, Philippa of Hainaut, who was French herself and whose pregnancy was far advanced, fell on her knees, and with tears in her eyes implored him: "Ah! my lord, since I have crossed the sea in great danger, I have never asked you any favor. But now I beg you, for the Son of the Blessed Mary and for the love of me, to have mercy on these six men!" The King could not refuse her and the six burghers of Calais were saved.

All these things and many others concerning the city were written in books of history by a Frenchman named Jean Froissart. He had been a protégé of Edward III and his kind Queen Philippa, and he told many tales of the wars that had been going on in France ever since the great siege of Calais. Froissart's histories were highly valued at Warwick Castle. The young boys in training there learned their lessons from Froissart. He told in his books how Richard Beauchamp's grandfather Thomas fought under the banner of Edward III at Crécy. In that famous battle the French, with fifteen thousand Genoese crossbowmen to help them, trampled each other underfoot and were slaughtered by a small but valiant English army. The English archers with their longbows let fly their arrows "as thick as snow" and the Genoese turned tail and fled. French horses and knights fell under that storm of arrows, and once down, the knights in their heavy armor could not rise again without help.

Meanwhile, the Black Prince, son of King Edward, and only sixteen years old, was hard pressed in another part of the field. Thomas Beauchamp fought at his side, protecting the gallant young man. At last he sent to the King for help, lest the Prince be overwhelmed by the enemy. But the King asked, "Is my son dead, or fallen, or so wounded that he cannot help himself?" And when he heard that the Prince was still alive, well, and fighting, he said, "Let the boy win his spurs." Then Thomas Beauchamp and the other lords around the Prince held their positions and performed even greater feats of valor until the victory of King Edward. There was a king! There was a prince! Under such leaders one Englishman could take on a dozen Frenchmen.

Ten years later they proved it again at Poitiers. The odds before this battle so favored the French that the Black Prince had actually offered to surrender the towns and castles he had captured during the current campaign, to set free all his French prisoners, and to keep the peace for the next seven years. But when King John of France refused the offer and the French gave battle, the English with their peerless archers cut down the flower of the chivalry of France and captured King John himself. Thomas Beauchamp was one of those who brought him as a prisoner to the tent of the Black Prince.

When, two generations later, Thomas Beauchamp's grandson Richard was appointed deputy Captain of Calais, the youth of England, Thomas Malory among them, were spoiling for another battle in which they could beat the French again as their grandsires had done at Crécy and at Poitiers. All they needed was another king like Edward III or another prince like the Black Prince. But their present King, Henry IV, was now a mental and physical ruin, subject to epileptic fits; his son, Prince Hal, was a scatterbrained ne'er-do-well. Some said that he had shown a grasp of the military arts when he served in putting down the Welsh rebellions, but England looked forward without enthusiasm to the accession of the young heir, and the King's death could not be far off.

This was how matters stood in 1414 as Richard Beauchamp prepared to leave for Calais. He would take with him a hundred men-at-arms and three hundred archers, men of Warwick already trained and tried in the fighting against the Welsh rebels. All were in good spirits and eager for the French adventure. They had been paid something toward their wages, and sooner or later, when the King paid the Earl for his services, they would receive more, besides booty, ransom money for prisoners, and rewards for valor following every victory. An attack on Calais by the French was expected and Richard Beauchamp's men hoped for it. Armor shining, banners flying, all emblazoned with the bear and the ragged staff, his mounted knights clattered through the stone gateway and thundered over the drawbridge of Warwick Castle. Minstrels with drums, pipes, and clarions led the men who followed on foot, the archers, and a long procession of servants. At the end came the baggage train of heavily loaded horses and ponies.

When they were gone, on their way to the coast, the Channel crossing, and France, the castle seemed empty, the courts silent, though in fact many men remained behind and the training of younger squires and pages went on as usual. Thomas and Philip grew expert in bouts with the quarterstaff and twice a week stripped to the waist for wrestling. Their bodies hardened to take the thudding of staves and fists bruising bare flesh. They became accustomed to the weight of heavy iron breastplates, the awkwardness of the pieces that protected arms and legs, the hollow darkness of the helmet lowered over the head. They learned all the strokes and cuts and thrusts of play with the blunted broadsword, the short sword, and the dagger. They experienced the stunning violence and deafening crash of a fall in a tournament, the wrenching effort to pull free from the stirrup and away from the iron-shod hooves of a galloping horse. They knew for the first time how an opponent looked when seen through the narrow slit of a closed helmet, sitting his horse like a statue of iron, then, at the sound of the clarion, tilting his lance, and suddenly looming, a bulk in a cloud of dust before the shattering shock of his blow dimmed the eyes.

There were other lessons too, leading the young squires into the mysteries of their high calling. The purpose of the knightly pilgrimage, the devotion to a lady, the quest in hope of seeing the Holy Grail in this life and of seeing God Himself in the life to come, all handed down since the days of King Arthur, were revealed. Thomas Malory wished passionately for the moment when he would kneel before the altar, dedicating his life to high and holy things. When would it come to pass? When would he feel the touch of Richard Beauchamp's sword on his shoulder and hear the voice of his good lord saying, "Rise, Sir Thomas Malory"? He longed to be knighted by the Earl of Warwick and no other man in the world.

Yet sometimes in Newgate Prison, when a cough or fever kept Thomas Malory restless at night, he dreamed that he was a boy again at Warwick Castle, creeping with Philip Chetwynd down stone steps to the dungeon where prisoners could be lodged. In the half-light the two boys would peer through bars at manacles and leg irons chained to the walls, and at the gibbet hanging from the ceiling where living bodies were left to rot, by order of the authorities. In a far corner was the awful darkness of the oubliette, the deep well where men were dropped to die, forgotten. Beyond the dungeon was a torture chamber which no page or squire ever saw. They simply knew that it was there for use when necessary, by order of the authorities. But who gave the authority? Did Richard Beauchamp give it? Did he know, or allow, or order what was done? Thomas Malory did not believe it. To the last day of his life he would not believe it. And yet the dungeon and the torture chamber were there. On uneasy nights the thought haunted him.

Then there was the troublesome matter of the Maid of Lorraine, burned at the stake in Rouen so many years ago. That was no fault of Richard Beauchamp. He had not watched while it was done. He had neither ordered it nor been able to stop it. And yet—

The best escape was to write. In the French book were the stories about Sir Launcelot, about his battles and his tournaments and his love for Arthur's Queen, Guinevere. Thomas Malory was putting them together in a new way and adding fancies of his own about the nature of true love.

"The month of May was come, when every lusty heart begins to blossom and to burgeon. For as trees and herbs burgeon and flourish in May, so every heart that is in any manner of lover springs forth, burgeons, buds and flourishes in lusty deeds. For it gives to all lovers desire, that merry month of May, more than any other month, and in wise lovers calls to their mind old courtesy and old service, and many kind deeds that they had forgotten . . ."

Kind deeds that they had forgotten . . . He had not forgotten his own May days with Elizabeth. Elizabeth Malory, a pretty name, and she had been a pretty bride. She was old now, still living at Newbold Revel. She sent him money when she could, and faithful letters. Once, so she told him, a hundred armed men had attacked the house when she was there with only a few servants. They had dragged her from the house and plundered it, making off with half his goods. It was not unusual. She could not even tell who they were—perhaps Yorkists, perhaps friends of Hugh Smyth, whose house Thomas Malory had once ransacked. Perhaps they were simply ruffians. Elizabeth had much to bear, her husband in prison off and on these twenty years, their son Robert dead. But she had always been a good manager. She kept things going at Newbold Revel and at their other properties. For the sake of little Nicholas, the grandson, she kept things going.

Elizabeth had tried long and hard for his release. It was always in vain, but the blast of the winter's wind had never withered her love and loyalty. He had not deserved such a woman. There must be a way to honor her. In the story of Tristram, he would change the name of Tristram's mother, a virtuous lady. He would call her not Isabelle but Elizabeth. In another story he had already added a character named Sir Hervis de Revel, a noble knight who "did marvelous deeds with King Arthur." Elizabeth and Revel, the two names should please his wife, if she ever saw his book.

She might never see it, but drawing a piece of paper toward him, he wrote:

As the biting wind of winter destroys the green summer, so it fares with unstable love in man and woman, for in many persons there is no stability; for we see every day how because of a little blast of winter's cold we discard true love that is so precious.

Therefore, as May flowers and flourishes in every man's garden, so let every man of honor open his heart in this world, first for God and then for those to whom he promised his faith. First devote yourself to the honor of God and then to the honor of your lady. I call this virtuous love . . .

But nowadays men cannot love seven nights without satisfying their desire. A love like that does not last, for heat soon cools. So goes love nowadays, soon hot, soon cold. This is no stability. But the old love was not so; then men and women could love for seven years without lust, and then was love truth and faithfulness. That was how love was in King Arthur's days.

He wrote of how Sir Launcelot loved Queen Guinevere with the true love that a knight owed to his lady. It was a love that would in the end destroy King Arthur and all the flower of knighthood. But before the end came, Launcelot would risk his life again and again to save the Queen. When she stood accused of treason and bound at the stake for trial by fire, he would come on a white charger, fight off her accusers, and carry her away to safety. That was how a noble knight should serve his lady. Guy of Warwick had done the same.

A wife of course might need different treatment. All men agreed that the wife ought to let her husband have the word and be master. But he had never needed to beat Elizabeth, and in time of danger he would have come to save her if he could.

Suddenly Thomas Malory, knight prisoner, saw in his mind what he feared to see. No one had come riding into the square at Rouen that long-ago day to save the Maid of Lorraine. She was indeed neither queen nor lady wife, but a peasant, a witch, and the destroyer of a kingdom. But Thomas Malory's eyes burned as if still seared with the flames he had seen that day at Rouen, and his ears still rang with the sound of her final cry, "Jesus!"

Could Richard Beauchamp have saved her? Should he have tried? No man is perfect. From his own imagining Thomas Malory was writing a story to pierce through to the heart of the matter. It was a story of a knight from Hungary, Sir Urry. He was wounded, and King Arthur with other kings and many knights tried to heal the wounds. But this was a feat that could be performed only by the best knight of the world. Sir Launcelot would not try because he was conscious of his sin. Then Sir Urry begged him to try for the love of God, and Sir Launcelot held up his hands and prayed that through him God would heal the wounds. Devoutly kneeling, he put his hands in the wounds so that they bled a little, and they were healed. "Then King Arthur, and all the kings and knights kneeled down and gave thanks and love to God and to his blessed mother, and Sir Launcelot wept as a child that had been beaten." It was a miracle of truth and forgiveness. God had sent the sign. In spite of his sin, Launcelot was still the best knight of the world. So it must have been with Richard Beauchamp.

There was but little space left at the end of his paper and the greatest of all the stories were yet to be told. He would begin on the other side of this sheet and hope that he could bribe the jailer to bring more paper tomorrow. Then, fall-

Launcelot

ing into French, as sometimes happened from old habit, he wrote: "On the other side follows the most piteous tale of the Morte Arthur Sans Guerdon par le chevalier sir Thomas Malory, knight. Jesu, aide lui pour votre bonne merci! Amen."

THE FRANCE OF THOMAS MALORY
ENGLAND
London
Bristol
Dover
Southampton
ENGLISH CHANNEL
Calais
Agincourt
Crécy
LORRAINE
Compiegne
Harfleur
Rouen
Meaux
Caen
Paris
NORMANDY
River
Seine
Troyes
BRITTANY
MAINE
Montereau
Orléans
Baugé
River Loire
BURGUNDY
Anjou
N
Poitiers

ARTHUR

> *"He shall be King and overcome all his enemies and before he dies he shall long be King of all England and have under his rule Wales, Ireland and Scotland and more realms than I will now tell."*
>
> THE TALE OF KING ARTHUR

IT was possible to escape from Newgate Prison. Thomas Malory remembered how a nobleman had escaped a dozen years ago, soon after being locked up for taking the wrong side in the civil wars. One of the jailers had got a horse and ridden away with him by night. Afterward, other prisoners had managed to get to the roof above the gate and to fend off the sheriffs who were sent to subdue them. They were brought down at last and laid in irons. But, like all prisoners, every man in Newgate whiled away hours of pain and tedium plotting to escape. Thomas Malory had escaped from other prisons, but it took skill, force, strength, money. He had none of these now.

It was possible to be pardoned and released from Newgate. Kings could pardon. They released felons, murderers, prisoners of war, even political enemies, but not Thomas Malory. The injustice of that refusal ate into his bone marrow. The charges against him were so many, so long ago, and the evidence so garbled, that he had never been brought to trial, never would be brought to trial. Only his name as a troublemaker and firebrand lingered on, even now when he was old and sick and almost friendless.

There was still one hope. Richard Beauchamp had been dead for thirty years, but Richard Neville, who had married Beauchamp's daughter, was now Earl of Warwick, and known as the "king-maker." His great house in Warwick Square was but a stone's throw from Newgate. The lay brother who brought the books from Greyfriars Abbey library promised to make a fair copy of each tale and carry the manuscripts to the Earl's house. He would persuade someone to show them to the Earl. With each packet of stories this powerful nobleman would see the name of the author and his plea for release from prison. Surely the Earl would find much in the tales to move him to pity for the knight prisoner.

Thomas Malory wrote of Sir Tristram, "who endured great pain . . . for sickness had overtaken him, and that is the greatest pain a prisoner may have. For all the while a prisoner may have his health of body he may endure under the mercy of God and in hope of good deliverance; but when sickness touches a prisoner's body, then may a prisoner say all wealth is him bereft, and then he hath cause to wail and weep."

And if this was not enough to move the present Earl of Warwick and his wife, in one tale after another Thomas Malory added family names to flatter them. They would like the story of how Sir Galahad met one Melias de Lisle and made him a knight, for Richard Beauchamp's first wife had been a de Lisle, and their daughter was the wife of Richard Neville. When they read the story of Sir Nerovens de Lisle, lieutenant of Pendragon Castle, they would remember when Sir William de Lisle of their own family had been deputy captain in the castle of Calais. It would please them to escape the grim present for happier memories of days when the name of Warwick meant honor and glory, the great days after Prince Hal reformed his ways and became the illustrious King Henry V. Harfleur and Agincourt would come to mind. Indeed, a Sir Launcelot de Lisle was one of the heroes whom Henry had rewarded with the captaincy of a French town after the victory at Agincourt.

The thought of Agincourt and all that led up to it made prison walls melt away. In memory Thomas Malory was a youth again, thirteen years old in the year when Henry IV suddenly and fortunately died. His son, Prince Hal, overwhelmed by his sense of the responsibility thrust upon him and by his own unworthiness for his new, exalted state, went at once to Westminster Abbey and spent the day kneeling in prayer. He received absolution from the hermit of Westminster, promised to amend his life, and dropped all his former wild friends and companions as if he had never known them.

There was much to repent. His father, Henry IV, had seized the throne from Richard II and ordered his murder. Henry V, soon to be crowned, now profited from his father's sin. Yet as a youth he had been knighted by the murdered Richard. His vows of fidelity to Richard, spoken at the high and holy altar, the sense of dedication to Richard's service, the vigils, the prayers of his young knighthood, all had been violated. For one entire day the new King did penance on his knees. He was also heir to an even more complex problem which he intended to solve with the help of his royal brothers as soon as he was safely crowned.

Richard Beauchamp returned from France to fulfill the duties of lord high steward for the solemn and glittering ceremonies. No one knew better than he how all details should be ordered. The coronation was to take place on April 9, 1413, in Westminster Abbey, and the Earl rode to London well ahead of that time with a great train of retainers, all splendid in silk and velvet, their robes edged with fur. Saddles and bridles were jewel-studded. Banners showing the bear and ragged staff rippled above the cavalcade as they set out from Warwick.

The young squire Thomas Malory burned to be with that retinue, to see the color and bustle of London town, to catch a glimpse of the King, perhaps even to be present in the Abbey when the crown was put on the royal brow and all the nobles of England shouted "God save the King!" But only knights and ladies of high rank were chosen to ride with the Earl to London.

When they returned to Warwick Castle they had much to say about the King. They spoke of his air of command, of his high color, of his bright eyes, of his white teeth and the attractive cleft in his chin. He was muscular, and when they saw him in armor, he seemed to wear it "as though it were a light cloak."

Among the banners which he flew was one bearing the arms of King Arthur, three golden crowns on a field of azure. It was a reminder of England's great past and a challenge for the future. The lords and ladies from Warwick returned ready to obey, respect, admire, even to adore King Henry.

Thomas Malory's place in the Earl's household was still a humble one, but he determined to advance in the King's service. His father was a Member of Parliament for Warwickshire this year, and that meant more money and influence. Sir John was making needed repairs and improvements at Newbold Revel. He had sent a horse to Thomas. The future looked bright. Thomas longed for a battle in which he could win his spurs by some act of heroism.

There was talk of a French expedition. This was the complex matter which occupied the King's mind. It was said that King Charles of France had sent a basket of tennis balls and some soft cushions to Henry as a hint that he was too young to play a man's part in the dangerous game of war. Whether or not this story was true, Henry had called on his lords of Church and State to prove to the people that their King had a right and duty to lead them to war against France. Henry's advisers found the documents that he wanted, showing beyond doubt that through a just inheritance all of western France should be his.

Ambassadors carried the message to France. Henry demanded Normandy, "which is his fully by right from the time of William I the Conqueror, though now, as of long time past, it has been withheld from him against God and all justice by the violence of the French." He claimed much more: the crown of France itself, and if that were refused, he claimed at the very least the territories ceded to Edward III by treaty after the battle of Poitiers. He also claimed the gold which France still owed for the ransom of

King John, captured at Poitiers almost sixty years ago. This debt amounted to the staggering sum of 1,600,000 French crowns. Finally, Henry demanded the hand of the French princess Catherine and a dowry of two million crowns.

It was a good time to make demands. King Charles VI of France was subject to periods of madness during which he thought that he was made of glass and would break if anyone came near him. At these times he was quite unfit to rule. Already, a large part of France was controlled by Armagnacs, followers of the Duke of Orléans, the King's brother. To the northeast in Flanders the Duke of Burgundy, the King's uncle, was another powerful threat.

At Henry's demand, French diplomats now came to Winchester. They did not want war. They offered territory, but not enough; they offered gold, but not enough. By the summer of 1413 all England knew that King Henry V intended to attack and take what France would not give.

More than once the Earl of Warwick returned home from Calais to raise money and find men to strengthen that key port and fortress. In time of peace he commanded Calais with thirty men-at-arms, thirty mounted archers, and four hundred foot soldiers. In time of war four times as many were needed. Even pages would be taken along to tend horses. Thomas Malory and Philip Chetwynd longed to be called. They felt their chins every morning for the first signs of a sprouting beard.

They watched bowstaves being made by the Earl's bowyers, arrows by the fletchers, and horseshoes by the farriers. Turners were at work on new wooden saddles, and carpenters were building carts for added transport. The Earl ordered every available horse to be readied except those needed in the harvest, and Sir John Malory sent his bailiff to bring in the horses owned by the tenants of Newbold Revel. The good old days of unpaid feudal service were over; now every man had to be paid or be owed the money for his services and his goods. Debts were written down in the bailiff's account book, and by autumn, flour, salted fish, and meat, as well as money, horses, and men, arrived at Warwick Castle on the first stage of the journey to the coast.

Guns were being made at the Tower of London; and at every port along the Channel, siege towers, scaling ladders, and battering rams were ready to load on ships and barges at the moment of command.

Day by day the great company of retainers at Warwick Castle dwindled as knights, squires, and pages were assigned to duty at Calais or elsewhere in the French adventure. In Lent of 1414 Philip Chetwynd, whose uncle Sir John Chetwynd was in the King's own retinue, received permission to ride the five miles from Warwick to Kenilworth Castle, where King Henry was making a royal visit. Philip returned to Warwick beside himself with excitement. Through family influence it had been arranged that he should join the French expedition as his uncle's squire.

Thomas wondered whether he and Philip would ever see each other again. He feared that his own family might beg the Earl to leave their son in England. But the French were expected to attack Calais and all of the best young men at Warwick were to go. Even now, old and sick as he was, Thomas Malory could smile as he remembered that he had been among those chosen as the best. He was assigned as one of three squires to Sir John Beauchamp, cousin of the Earl of Warwick. His duties were to tend his lord's armor and weapons, to find and serve his food, to guard his horses, carry his messages.

Still smiling, the knight prisoner dipped his pen into the inkhorn and wrote about a knight of King Arthur's Round Table: "He was poor and poorly arrayed. He did not put himself forward. But in his heart he was fully assured that he would do as well, if fortune favored him, as any knight that was there." How hopeful and ambitious Thomas Malory had been in his fourteenth year!

He remembered the long ride to the south coast through Oxford and Winchester, bypassing London, where a plague was raging. At Winchester the men from Warwick stopped for a supply of bread freshly baked to feed them on their journey to Calais. The castle at Winchester easily housed all of the Earl of Warwick's men and Thomas Malory saw there for the first time the Round Table of King Arthur. It hung on the wall, a great circle of oak, dark with age. According to tradition, Winchester had once been Camelot, and here was the proof. Geoffrey of Monmouth had said that King Arthur's second battle against Mordred was fought at Winchester. To Thomas Malory this was a holy place.

The following day the cavalcade went on to Southampton. Men-at-arms, the "lances," and the archers both mounted and on foot, the strings of horses with their grooms, squires, and pages moved toward the adventure and the gold that lay ahead in France. Several of the King's crowns, many jewels, ornaments, even the rich vestments and holy relics of the royal chapel had been signed away as pledges of future payment for the troops.

Arthur

In his prison cell, Thomas Malory's smile took on an ironic twist. He had never been fully paid. But it was not the fault of King Henry V. If the King had lived, all would have been paid. His steadfastness, his sense of order, his passion for justice would have changed the world and saved it from the chaos that came later. England would have ruled the world. Now she could not even rule herself.

From Southampton the fleet bearing the men of Warwickshire sailed to reinforce Calais. Among knights, squires, and pages, Thomas Malory crowded into the place assigned to him. Men, horses and baggage, and machines of war all were distributed as evenly as possible for balance and weight. The weather was fine and a fair wind blew as the ships rounded the south coast in a week of sailing. At Dover the men went on shore for a last night on English soil before crossing to Calais. Here Arthur too had once set sail for France, so the stories told, his ships studding the sea with white sails. Dover Castle still crowned the cliffs as it had done in Arthur's day. Built and rebuilt from that time to this, Dover Castle guarded the straits on the English coast as fortified Calais did on the French side.

Calais, held by the English since the great siege of 1346, was still "the key to France." But now the long uneasy truce was about to be broken. As England saw it, France was flinging down the gauntlet, preparing to recapture Calais, which mad King Charles dared to call his own. Henry V of England thought otherwise, and gave his reasons. The French King replied that Henry could never rule on French soil and that he was not even the legitimate King of England because he was not descended from Richard II.

Nevertheless, Henry was determined to unite the two countries once and for all. His trusted Captain of Calais,

Richard Beauchamp, would repel the French attack and strengthen the fortifications while Henry completed preparations for his own assault on the French mainland. To Thomas Malory in his ardent youth it was as if he were about to join and serve Sir Launcelot before King Arthur came to win his ancient victories in France.

Richard Beauchamp's men found the Channel crossing hard, though a following wind favored the fleet all day. The month was December, the sea was rough. The ships pitched and tossed, and the young, like Thomas, new to saltwater sailing, looked out with dull seasick eyes as Dover Castle faded into the misty horizon and the faint line of the French coast appeared. Who would meet them on that shore—friend or foe? In their weakness and misery, how could they land against enemy forces?

But after all, there was no enemy to meet. They saw English flags flying from the fortress of Calais. Friendly English hands helped to beach and tie up the ships, to lower gangplanks and push or pull nervous horses to shore. Sir John Beauchamp and his retinue were given quarters in the castle of Calais. Others occupied houses of the citizens. Calais was cramped, but for the moment food was plentiful and the news was good. Danger of an attack had passed.

This being so, Richard Beauchamp was preparing to celebrate the Yuletide at Guines, where there was an ancient castle not far from Calais. There both English and French champions, forgetting their more serious differences for the festive season, were issuing challenges to feats of chivalry.

The day appointed was the Twelfth Day of Christmas, a time when, as stories told, King Arthur had liked to see his knights engage in adventures. True to that tradition, Richard Beauchamp now ordered three shields to be decorated with paintings of ladies in charming poses—playing a harp, embroidering, making a chaplet of flowers.

Thomas Malory would have given anything he possessed to see the splendid tournament at Guines. He was not chosen to go. He only saw the Earl's company riding out from Calais, their mantles emblazoned with the bear and ragged staff. Other squires, not he, stood at the end of the lists tending the horses on the first great day. They told Thomas what he had missed and he saw the glorious combat in his mind's eye. Even now in his old age it was as vivid as ever.

On the first day of the tournament at Guines, Richard Beauchamp's helmet was topped with a plume of ostrich feathers. Like a knight of legend he rode into the field, his visor closed so that no one recognized him as the Earl of Warwick. He easily unhorsed his opponent, a French knight clad in red armor. The next day, his visor again hiding his face, he defeated a knight in white armor and was greatly applauded. On the last day of the jousting, the Earl rode into the lists with his visor open so that all knew who he was. Around his helmet he wore a circlet of pearls and precious stones. He carried his third shield and bore the Beauchamp coat of arms. Clarions and kettledrums sounded a fanfare.

On this day he sat his horse so firmly under his opponent's strong blows that the French said he must be strapped to his saddle. To prove the contrary, Richard Beauchamp leaped from his horse and remounted. Then, having defeated the last of his gallant opponents, he gave handsome steeds and other rich gifts to all three, and rode back to Calais amid cheering crowds.

KNIGHT PRISONER

Now, long afterward in his dark cell, Thomas Malory wrote of that great and colorful tournament as if he saw it blazing with light, and as if the three battles had been fought by himself, Gareth, the generous-handed, disguised as Beaumains, "the kitchen knight." But "Beaumains" was also a disguise for the name of Beauchamp; Thomas Malory told how Beaumains fought and defeated a knight in black armor, and a green knight, and a red knight, as Richard Beauchamp had chivalrously fought and defeated the three knights at Guines. This was how things once had been, and should be. It was chivalry at its best.

The name and fame of Richard Beauchamp were already known to the illustrious Emperor Sigismund, whose power and influence extended over the Holy Roman Empire. This great ruler met Beauchamp in 1414, gave him a jeweled sword, and offered an even more precious object, the heart of St. George, as a gift to the English King. St. George, born in the Holy Land, had been made patron saint of England by Edward III. The Earl persuaded the Emperor Sigismund to come himself to England with the holy relic and to receive the personal thanks of King Henry V.

Sigismund was so much impressed by Richard Beauchamp's character and graceful manner that he said of him, "No Christian prince has a knight equal to him for wisdom, culture, and manhood. If all courtesy were lost, it could be found again in him." The words might have been used to describe Launcelot. Thomas Malory's devotion to his lord grew even deeper.

The meeting of Richard Beauchamp and the Emperor Sigismund involved much more than an exchange of gifts and token honors. The new King Henry had employed the

Earl in the distasteful duty of putting down religious heresy at home. Now Henry chose him as the right man to understand and give his personal judgment on the spreading of heresy abroad. Meetings on this vital subject were being held at a council in Constance, an important city of the Holy Roman Empire. Richard Beauchamp would be the representative of the English King.

Accompanied by a brilliant escort of knights, bishops, and learned doctors, the Earl soon left Calais for Constance, where Sigismund had called together the best minds of all Christian countries. Their first aim was to make a fresh start in the affairs of the Church, which had fallen into a sad state. At this time no less than three popes claimed the authority to head the Church; somehow the schism must be ended. A few radical minds were proposing as a second goal the reform of the Church itself, perhaps even by subordinating the papacy and eliminating the college of cardinals, which elected popes.

The third matter of concern at Constance was to stamp out the heresy promoted by one John Huss, a disciple of the earlier English heretic John Wycliffe. These dangerous men believed that the Church should be separated from the State and that the Bible contained all the truth man needed for salvation. Wycliffe had even dared translate the Bible into English so that his countrymen could read the Holy Scriptures for themselves.

Wycliffe, the firebrand, had died quietly in bed, but the fires still burned, and Richard Beauchamp's efforts to stamp them out were being carried on by others in England. Wycliffe's followers, known as Lollards, were being tortured, hanged, even burned at the stake. Now it appeared that John Huss, "the Bohemian Wycliffe," was about to suffer the same fate. On July 6, 1415, the second year of the reign of Henry V, John Huss was burned at the stake in the square before the cathedral at Constance.

Richard Beauchamp was spared the pain of witnessing that event. At Calais his men learned that their lord had returned to England to help the King prepare his long-expected invasion of France. Already Henry had gathered two thousand men-at-arms and six thousand archers, with another thousand military specialists. Physicians, heralds, and minstrels would accompany the King, as well as men of the Church, some of whom would write the history of the campaign. All these men were assembling in the harbors of England's south coast. The King worked tirelessly, attending to all details, visiting the ships, writing notes in English that his craftsmen could understand.

The King's political actions were also clear and easy to understand. Just before the time set for sailing, a plot to murder him was discovered. The conspirators were quickly brought to trial and quickly executed. On August 11, a Sunday, Henry set sail from Portsmouth. His flagship, the *Trinity Royal*, with a crew of three hundred, was surrounded, as it sailed out of the harbor, by an escort of swans, a sure sign of heaven's blessing on the fleet. Henry reminded his friends and courtiers of words that had been spoken by Richard II in knighting him: "Be gallant and bold, for unless you conquer, you will have little name for valor." Henry IV on his deathbed had given his son similar advice: "Do not let your kingdom remain too long at peace." Power for the English King, honor for England, riches for its people lay ahead on the French coast. To the sound of drums and trumpets, and with prayers to God, the fleet took to the sea.

Arthur

This time Henry was not moving toward Calais. His sails were bent southward toward Harfleur, at the mouth of the Seine. He intended to open the walls of Harfleur and make of it another Calais as a second key to France. Some of the English forces at Calais were ordered to meet and assist the King on his landing.

So it was that Thomas Malory, now in his fifteenth year, sailed with Sir John Beauchamp and a body of his men from Calais along the coast of Picardy and Normandy. They commandeered small boats and barges along their route. Early in August they reached Harfleur and saw that the people of the city had flooded the fields to the north. The French commander, Sire de Gaucourt, was strengthening his forces against the expected English attack. He had raised defensive earthworks, but for some reason these were unmanned. With the men of Warwickshire Thomas Malory landed safely and camped in a field west of Harfleur. They worked mightily to prepare for the King's arrival.

On August 13 they saw the fleet, first one white sail, then three, then a dozen, until countless sails converged on the point of land west of Harfleur. The fleet numbered fifteen hundred vessels. Anchors were dropped from the biggest ships, and Richard Beauchamp's men put out in small boats to bring in soldiers, horses, and baggage. Other ships were pulled to the beach so that men on board could leap into the shallow water and wade to shore.

But the King held back his eager troops. In the dark before dawn of the following day, August 14, only a few of his most trusted leaders came ashore, mounted, to explore. They chose a position on a hill above Harfleur and sent word to the King. Then, with the sun shining and the morning beautiful, Henry V was rowed to shore. He knelt to pray for a moment on the beach and moved on purposefully to occupy his hillside headquarters. The full army of thirty thousand men followed, grouping themselves around Harfleur. The landing went on for three days.

King Henry spent his nights in a nearby priory and a few of his nobles found shelter in houses abandoned by the fleeing French country people, but most of the great army set up tents or slept in the open fields and orchards around Harfleur. For many, it was the first experience of "living off the land." In orchards, fruit was hanging thick, although it was not yet ripe. The English soldiers ate it when they could find nothing else. They drank from the river that flowed into and out of the town. They also drank raw new wine stolen from French cellars.

From the city's walls the French garrison shot volleys of stone and flights of flaming arrows at the invaders. The soldiers of the English artillery sweated under the August sun. Outside Harfleur's moat they set guns and catapults in place, but the English toll of dead and wounded began even before they could mount their attack on the city.

Many men who were waiting idle in the heat threw off their stifling armor and went to look for food and plunder. They burned farmhouses, they took women as prisoners and brought them into the English camps. From his silk tent on the hillside above Harfleur King Henry saw his men marauding. He seemed to see everything that happened, day or night. He set severe punishments for robbing churches, for pillaging, and for offenses against women. The sentence for killing or raping a woman was death. A man endangering the life of a pregnant woman in

Arthur

any way was to lose his possessions and to die unless pardoned by the King. Any woman who came as a prostitute to the English camps was to be warned once. If she came again, she would be sent home with a broken arm.

Thomas Malory had his first taste of war at Harfleur. He saw the corpses of men lying by the guns and catapults. He saw what had been stolen from French houses—money, clothing, bits of furniture. It would be easy to steal something for himself. But the sight of the King's tent on the hill deterred him. So did the knowledge that a first theft would make a second one easier. He feared to become corrupt, unfit for knighthood.

By August 19 Harfleur was surrounded by the English artillery. King Henry called on the French garrison to surrender. He warned, almost begged them to spare their women and children the horrors of war. When their commander refused, the bombardment began.

Rocks soaked in oil or tar flew blazing from the catapults and hurtled over the walls, setting fires and causing panic among the people. A ceaseless cannonade of rocks crashed with a frightful noise against the walls or tore great holes in them. Day and night the guns roared. The walls of Harfleur were crumbling faster than the French defenders could rebuild them. Within a month the English soldiers could come close enough to fill parts of the moat and set scaling ladders against the walls. The French commander then surrendered the city.

King Henry's terms were harsh. He had lost many men, dead or wounded. Great numbers of men lay deadly sick of the bloody flux. The heat, the unripe fruit and raw wine, the dirty water and swarming flies had destroyed a large part of the English army while they were destroying Harfleur. Furthermore, said the King, Harfleur was *his* city and its destruction was the fault of its stubborn citizens. Therefore, they must take an oath of obedience to King Henry or leave Harfleur and be replaced by Englishmen. Two thousand of the poor and the old, the women, children, and priests were to be sent away, permitted to take with them nothing but small bundles. Even outside the walls their weeping and lamenting could be heard, but there was no help for it; Harfleur would now be a garrison town where such people could not live.

Before all these orders could be carried out, there were ceremonies to set a seal on the surrender of Harfleur. On the Sunday after the fall of the city, Thomas Malory saw the military leaders of Harfleur coming out through the battered gate with twenty-four other hostages. They were on their way to undergo the same humiliation which Edward III had put upon the six men of Calais. They wore the white robes of penitents and had ropes around their necks. They climbed the hill to the King's headquarters. The whole English army soon learned what happened there. The defeated Frenchmen were made to move from tent to tent, kneeling for a long time in each as they waited in vain for the King to come. Finally, they were led into his own tent, where they saw him sitting on a throne draped with cloth of gold and surrounded by his nobles. Again the men of Harfleur knelt while King Henry refused even to look at them. At last he demanded the keys to the city and received them. He said that the people of Harfleur were much to blame because they had refused for a month to give him his own city. Then, as a sign of his mercy, he feasted the hostages royally and sent them home.

After this, thirty-two chaplains and a bishop, all robed in

Arthur

silk and cloth of gold and served by thirty-two squires, marched into Harfleur with lighted torches to celebrate Mass in the church of St. Martin. But King Henry entered the city in simple dress. He took off his shoes at the gate where English flags now flew and walked barefoot to the church. There he prayed and gave thanks for his victory.

In King Henry's retinue chaplains, clerks, chroniclers, and minstrels were recording the story of the siege and the victory. They wrote in French, in Latin, and in English, so that all men might know what all men, both French and English, had felt at Harfleur. One chronicler put it best of all when he wrote that after Harfleur King Henry "was so dreaded and feared by his princes and knights, captains and all kinds of people, that there was no one, however near and dear to him, that dared break his ordinances, especially his English subjects; and those of the kingdom of France who were under his obedience, whatever their rank, were equally reduced to this." It was as if Arthur had come again.

King Henry V was vividly in his mind as Thomas Malory in his prison cell at Newgate began to write *The Noble Tale of King Arthur and the Emperor Lucius*. He wrote of how King Arthur claimed the title of Roman Emperor by right of descent and of how he appeared to the Roman ambassadors, "in his state, which was the royalest that ever we saw . . . and in his person the most manly man that liveth, and is likely to conquer all the world, and even that is too little for his courage." He told how King Arthur set sail for France with a great multitude of ships "till they arrived at Barflete in Flanders, and when they were there he found many of his great lords ready as they had been commanded to wait upon him." Then he wrote how a city was besieged with "rearing of ladders, breaking of walls, and the ditch filled" and of how when the city was won "the duke's eldest son brought out the keys, and kneeling, delivered them to the king and asked him for mercy . . . Then came the king upon a hill, and saw the city and his banner on the walls. And he commanded that none of his liege men should misuse a lady, wife, or maid."

He wrote of King Arthur's many victories against the Romans and how afterward he "gave lands and realms unto his servants and knights, to each one as he deserved, so that none complained, rich or poor," and brought his men rejoicing home to England. Thomas Malory ended *The Noble Tale of King Arthur and the Emperor Lucius* on that note of triumph, as well he might. But in his memory, and in the memory of all Englishmen, after the victory at Harfleur came Agincourt.

King Henry had lost a third of his army at Harfleur. Another thousand men had to be kept there to repair the walls and garrison the town. Any ordinary leader would have set sail at once for England, and his councilors advised him to do just this. But Henry was no ordinary man. He sent the wounded, the sick, and many of his prisoners to England under the command of Richard Beauchamp, while he himself determined to march with his remaining soldiers north along the coast to Calais.

"For," he said, "I am possessed with a burning desire to see my territories and the places which ought to be my inheritance. If I should depart, they would reproach me that I suddenly fled, and lost what is mine by right through the appearance of fear. We will go, if it pleases God, without harm or danger, and if they disturb our journey, we shall come off with victory, triumph, and very great fame." Then he sent a messenger to Calais asking that a further detachment of men should be sent to guard the ford near the mouth of the river Somme, where he intended to cross. Those who had come from Calais to meet him would return with him, increasing somewhat his meager force of men.

Before setting out on his march, Henry wrote a letter to the Dauphin, the heir to the French throne. He challenged the young man, then nineteen years of age, to single combat, the victor to be King of France on the death of the ailing Charles VI. "It is better for us, cousin," wrote Henry, "to decide this war forever between our two persons." France and England were two Christian countries, he said. They should unite rather than destroy one another. Henry waited eight days for an answer. No answer came. On October 8, 1415, the march to Calais began.

Riding at the rear of the cavalcade was a priest, a chaplain of the King, whose duty was to make notes of all that happened on the campaign. He was a Frenchman, a native of Aquitaine, and his name was Master John de Bordin. Thomas Malory, also at the rear, riding with the armor of Sir John Beauchamp, saw the learned chaplain at work each night with tablet of paper and pen in hand, recording the events of the day. He was never to know how Master de Bordin came to be with King Henry V. Perhaps it was simply because Aquitaine was under English control in those days. Perhaps Master de Bordin admired the English King and had attached himself to Henry's court as Jean Froissart had done at the court of Edward III. In later years Richard Beauchamp had owned a copy of Master de Bordin's history; Thomas Malory read the famous document.

Through its pages he recalled the hunger, the fear, and the fatigue of the march to Calais. Only the King's presence, his great spirit and his concern for his men had made each day bearable. When they met resistance from towns along their route, King Henry offered to pass peacefully in exchange for a supply of good bread and wine. When they came to small rivers, he directed his scouts to find the safest places for wading across them.

So with few casualties the army moved northward until October 13. They were hoping to cross the Somme the next day. "But," wrote Master de Bordin, "it was suddenly told us by our scouts and advanced guard of horse that a great part of the French army was on the opposite side of the river to prevent our crossing." The reinforcement from Calais had already been intercepted by the French and forced to retreat.

Henry therefore turned east and led his army along the Somme, watching for a safe place to cross farther up the river. From time to time they were attacked by small bands of French soldiers, and even the common people came against them with hatchets and mallets. As a result, Henry took prisoners and learned from them why King Charles had not yet launched a full-scale attack. The French King feared that if he moved a large force westward, the Duke of Burgundy might seize the chance to occupy unprotected territory. Now, however, the French were ready to give battle against Henry. They considered the English archers to be the chief threat and would send thousands of armed horsemen against them.

Hearing this, King Henry ordered "that each archer should provide himself with a pole, six feet in length and sharp at each end, so that whenever the French cavalry should attack, these poles would be fixed in the ground sloping toward the enemy and both horses and horsemen be forced to retreat for fear of being thrown on them."

On October 19 King Henry was able to lead his weary army to two causeways which crossed the river Somme. The approach was through low swampy ground and the King himself helped to direct the crossing so that his tired and fearful men would not crowd the narrow passages. The boys with the baggage waited in the mud of the swamp until almost nightfall before they were allowed to cross. But each one, as he passed along the causeway, saw the King's calm and cheerful face and felt that all would be well. That night they slept soundly in farmhouses left by the French. Within a week they should reach Calais if the French did not harass them.

But the next day three French heralds arrived and demanded to see the King. They came from the Duke of Orléans and the Duke of Bourbon, allies of King Charles and commanders of the French army. King Henry met them on horseback in an open field where they knelt and told him formally that many French lords were assembled to do battle with him before he reached Calais.

Henry replied, "Be all things according to the will of God." When the heralds asked what road he intended to take, he answered, "Straight to Calais, and if our adversaries attempt to stop us, it will be at their own peril. We will not seek to meet them, nor will we move faster or slower because of them. But tell them not to interrupt our journey unless they wish to spill much Christian blood." He then gave the heralds a hundred pieces of French gold and dismissed them courteously.

On October 24 the army of English men-at-arms with their archers and their baggage, about six thousand men in all, crossed a little river called the Ternoise near the town of Blangy. On the far side of the river they climbed a hill and looked down into a valley. There they saw the French army. As de Bordin wrote: "We saw three columns of the French emerge from the upper part of the valley, about a mile from us. Being formed into battalions, companies, and troops, in multitudes compared with us, they halted a little more than half a mile away, filling a very wide field, as with an innumerable host of locusts."

King Henry spoke to his army with great courteousness and courage. He conferred knighthood upon a number of his commanders. The night came on and it was too dark to see anything except a narrow white road along the hilltop, but this road led to the village of Maisoncelles, where they found the best food they had eaten for many a day. Afterward, by the King's order, they lighted their fires and rested quietly, but the King went from one fire to another, talking to his men, seeing that all had made their confessions to a priest and that the archers were fitting new strings to their bows. In the field below they saw the French campfires and heard shouting. The French were in high spirits and were playing at dice for the prisoners they expected to take. It began to rain.

In the morning the sun shone, but the low ground where the French were camped was a sea of mud, churned by the all-night trampling of their many horses. Their battle line of heavily armed knights was crowded between two small woods near the town of Agincourt, with their horsemen on either side and behind them.

King Henry formed his archers into a wedge facing the French and told them to drive their poles into the ground before them. He also told them that the French had sworn to cut off three fingers of any archer they captured. The English horsemen flanked the archers, but because they were few, they were not crowded together as the French were. The King rode along the lines. He was mounted on a white horse decorated with the richest trappings, his armor caught the sun's rays. His surcoat was half blue, embroidered with the French fleur-de-lis, and half red, embroidered with the three golden leopards of England. His head was bare so that all could see his confident, resolute face. Then he put on his helmet, circled with a jeweled golden crown.

One of Henry's knights said to him that he wished the English army were larger. To this the King replied, "Truly I do not wish it. If we won a victory with an army as large as the enemy's, we might think that we had won through our own strength. If we were defeated, the bigger the army, the greater the loss. But if we win with so few men, we will know that God has given us the victory." He reminded his men that this day, October 25, was the feast of St. Crispin and St. Crispinian and said that this day would be remembered forever.

Thomas Malory rode forward with other squires to arm the knights whom they attended, but Sir John Beauchamp ordered him to return his horse to the rear. By the King's command, most of the knights were to fight on foot against the host of French knights mounted on horseback.

An hour passed. Two hours. All morning long the two armies faced each other, the French so crowded together in their front ranks that they saw they would not be able to wield their long lances for either offense or defense. They broke off the shafts to shorten them. At last, tired of waiting, they sat down on the ground to eat and drink.

The English had no food and they were not likely to get any. If they did not fight soon, they would fall from hunger and weakness. At eleven o'clock King Henry gave the order for attack.

The marshal in command threw his baton into the air and the King shouted, "Banners advance, in the name of Jesus, Mary, and St. George!" The archers quickly knelt. Each made the sign of the cross on the ground and kissed it, taking a little earth into his mouth as a token that he was prepared to die. The English trumpets sounded and the archers moved forward at an even pace, carrying their poles.

They were dirty and ragged, protected only by their leather jackets. Some were barefoot. They were tired, and many had been sick. But with a cry of "St. George!" they marched steadily toward the French host until they were within firing range.

At Maisoncelles the squires heard the trumpets and the shouts of the advancing archers. The King's chaplain rode toward the crest of the hill to view the battle. Some of the squires rode with him to join the action if they could. Thomas Malory was one of these. Only a handful remained behind to guard the baggage, which included much treasure belonging to the King, but a glorious chance for knighthood lay ahead on the battlefield.

Looking down from the top of the hill, Thomas Malory saw the archers driving their sharpened stakes into the ground. He saw them drawing their bows and taking aim. There was a sound like the rushing of water over a dam and the air was darkened with a storm of arrows, flight after flight.

With a defiant shout the French horsemen rode forward, their heads down to protect their faces from the constant stream of deadly arrows. Many fell. Others galloped straight at the sharp stakes, where their horses were gashed and threw their riders to the ground. French men-at-arms on foot now came gallantly forward into the melee and were trampled by horses who reared and turned back, maddened with fear.

The English archers regrouped and attacked from both sides. When they had driven the French men-at-arms toward the center, they dropped their bows, drew hatchets and mallets from their belts, and ran forward to kill the fallen. Many picked up swords and lances dropped by the French, who lay dead or suffocating under heaps of the wounded and slain.

In the thick of the fray King Henry fought against the most valiant of the French nobles. A score of these gallant knights could be seen battling their way toward the English King to kill him or to die in the attempt. Thomas Malory saw a French battle-ax raised above the King's head. He saw it crash down upon the helmet with the golden crown. Then the King's lance pierced French armor and his opponent disappeared among the English guards who closed in around their King.

Within three hours many thousands of French men-at-arms had been killed or wounded. Hundreds of noble prisoners had been taken, and all of them would be worth large ransoms to their English captors. Every available English soldier was called in to disarm the prisoners and to guard them. Seeing his squires, Sir John Beauchamp called them to this duty. Thomas Malory was called. He remembered his pride as he received the sword of a noble French captive, who stood with his head bowed, his face distorted by shame and grief.

The din of battle was dying down. But now other French knights were seen forming into columns as if about to renew the attack. If this happened, would the prisoners seize weapons and join their countrymen against the nearly exhausted English?

Thomas Malory saw the English military commanders clustered around the King, who had withdrawn from the center of the field. Then there was a flurry and messengers spread out with an order: "Kill the prisoners!" The English men-at-arms greeted this command with disbelief. Kill the prisoners! That meant going home almost as empty-handed as they had come. To disobey the King was unthinkable, but this time he had asked too much. Only a few obeyed.

While the issue was still in doubt, a squire came running down the hill and knelt trembling at the King's feet. His message was soon reported over the battlefield. A rabble of several hundred French peasants, led by three knights, had appeared from nowhere and had plundered the baggage at Maisoncelles. They had killed several of the squires on guard there and made off with horses, gold, silver, and, worst of all, with a crown and precious jeweled sword belonging to the King.

A moment later another order was sent out to the English men-at-arms. The prisoners must be killed without delay. Any knight who refused would lose his horse. Any man of lesser rank would lose his right ear. The killing of

Arthur

the prisoners began. Thomas Malory killed the unknown French knight whom he was guarding. He ran him through the neck with the sword that had been surrendered to him.

As night fell and it began to rain again, the dark figures of French peasants moved about among the thousands of dark and silent dead, finishing the work started by the English soldiers. They stripped the pale bodies of their countrymen, leaving them naked on the field. But at Maisoncelles the English dead, less than a hundred, were placed in an empty barn with much armor, clothing, and useless loot, for the King had ordered that no man might bring away with him more than he could carry. The barn was set on fire. Only the bodies of two men received special honors; these were the Duke of York, who was the King's uncle, and the young Earl of Suffolk, whom he admired. Their corpses were boiled and the flesh removed, so that the bones could be taken home to England.

In later years Thomas Malory often dreamed of Agincourt. Strangely enough, he saw it in his dreams not as the great victory it had been, far greater than Crécy and Poitiers. When he came to write of it in Newgate Prison, he saw in his mind the King fighting in mortal danger. And he saw the dead.

> There was but rushing and riding, foining and striking, and many a grim word was there spoken either to other, and many a deadly stroke. But ever King Arthur rode throughout the battle of Sir Mordred many times and did full nobly, as a noble king should do, and at all times he faltered never . . . And thus they fought all the day long, and never stinted, till the noble knights were laid to the cold ground, and ever they

fought still, till it was near night, and by then was there an hundred thousand laid dead upon the earth.

No one had ever counted the dead at Agincourt, how many French, how many English. When they were dead and stripped naked, they all looked alike.

Then King Arthur looked about and was aware where stood Sir Mordred leaning upon his sword among a great heap of dead men . . . "Now tide me death, tide me life," said the king, "now I see him yonder alone, he shall never escape my hands! For at a better advantage shall I never have him."
"God speed you well!" said Sir Bedivere.
Then the king got his spear in both his hands, and ran toward Sir Mordred, crying and saying, "Traitor, now is thy death day come!"
And when Sir Mordred saw King Arthur he ran unto him with his sword drawn in his hand, and there King Arthur smote Sir Mordred under the shield, with a foin of his spear, throughout the body more than a fathom. And when Sir Mordred felt that he had his death wound, he thrust himself with the might that he had up to the bur of King Arthur's spear, and right so he smote his father, King Arthur, with his sword held in both his hands, upon the side of the head, that the sword pierced the helmet and the skull. And therewith Mordred fell down stark dead to the earth.

On the table before him Thomas Malory had a copy of the old poem *Le Morte Arthur*. He had heard it many times in his childhood, thinking of the heroic stories of Crécy and Poitiers. Perhaps that poet too had thought of long-ago battles as he wrote. But Agincourt was the same. It was of Agincourt that Thomas Malory thought now.

Then heard they people cry in the field.

"Now go thou, Sir Lucan," said the king, "and find out for me what betokens that noise in the field."

So Sir Lucan departed, for he was grievously wounded in many places; and so as he went he saw and harkened by the moonlight how that plunderers and robbers were come into the field to plunder and rob many a full noble knight of brooches and bracelets and of many a good ring and many a rich jewel. And who that were not dead all out, there they slew them for their harness and their riches.

Then there was the matter of the sword, the precious sword that had disappeared when the plunderers came to Maisoncelles after the battle at Agincourt. The poet of *Le Morte Arthur* had written of how Excalibur disappeared— "that noble sword, and the pommel and the haft was all precious stones." At the command of the dying King Arthur, Sir Bedivere took it to the water's side.

And there he bound the girdle about the hilt, and threw the sword as far into the water as he might. And there came an arm and a hand above the water, and took it and grasped it, and shook it thrice and brandished it, and then vanished with the sword into the water.

Thomas Malory reread what he had written and knew with certainty that he had told this part of the story well, better than anyone had told it before. Since starting his task so long ago, his writing had gained a sure touch. He was adding with confidence what he knew would please the Earl of Warwick, but he was also adding what suffering had taught him. And as he reread, he found that he had told what he himself did not understand until he put it on paper. It had to do with the life and death of kings.

GUINEVERE

"As for our most noble King Arthur, we love him and honor him as well as you do, but as for Queen Guinevere, we love her not, because she is a destroyer of good knights."
        THE BOOK OF LAUNCELOT AND QUEEN GUINEVERE

THE inmates of Newgate called it the Press Yard, but it was not quite certain how the prison had earned this name. Some prisoners said that there was or had been a room where a man could be fastened to a board and loaded with weights until he confessed what his jailers wanted him to confess, or was pressed to death. Others said that the "Press Yard" simply meant the "House of Oppression."

    When Thomas Malory had first come to Newgate, he had been thrown into the hold for condemned men. He paid for a candle, which was handed to him through the small hatch in the heavy door, and saw a dark room, below ground, with walls and floor of stone, spattered with filth. A powerful stench sickened him. He saw chains fixed to hooks in the walls and iron staples driven into the ground to bring to due submission those who were stubborn and unruly. Two boards served for a bed.

The next day a prisoner called advice to him from a nearby cell, and he learned that he could pay to be moved to a better room. He soon found himself in the "better room" with thieves and other villains. They slept two or three to a bed and passed their time in a losing battle against disease and vermin. Some of the men were stupid, some were clever. Many, like Thomas Malory, were political prisoners. He made a friend of one lively rogue who called himself a "Brother of the Quill." He had written a broadside against the present government of King Edward IV and earned a year in Newgate as a reward.

Others whom Thomas Malory met during his first months at Newgate were quiet fellows imprisoned for crimes of passion. They had reconciled themselves to living in jail and even claimed to have been reformed by prison life. Their wives came to visit them and a few of the men had fathered children while serving a sentence. For a long while Elizabeth too had come to visit, bringing food, a warm cloak, a blanket, and money. None of these comforts lasted, because the prisoners in the common room stole from each other.

At last Thomas Malory was given a cell with one other man, an old soldier named Thomas Hostell who had been at Harfleur and at Agincourt. The two men spent many hours in talk of those great victories and in debate over what had gone wrong with their lives afterward. Was it only a turn of Fortune's wheel, which every man must expect? Or was the Yorkist King Edward IV a damned coldhearted villain who could never forgive a Lancastrian? Hostell was in prison for debt, only for debt, and he wrote to

King Edward asking for a pardon. He described his wounds, received in the service of King and country—an eye lost at Harfleur, a leg shattered at Agincourt—and he begged to be forgiven his debts. He was still waiting for an answer when he died. After Hostell's death Thomas Malory had the cell to himself and his memories.

On the night following the battle of Agincourt, news had spread through the army that King Henry was dining in state, waited upon by his most distinguished captives, the Duke of Orléans and the Duke of Bourbon. This ceremony was deeply satisfying to the fighting men when they heard about it. It was a symbol of the victory they had won for their King.

On October 26 they started toward Calais, every man and every horse heavily loaded with the spoils of war. The going was hard and the food scanty. At Guines, where Richard Beauchamp had performed his feats of chivalry the year before, King Henry decided to show his captives the mercy of a gracious sovereign by inviting them to rest in the old castle.

He sent the army on ahead to Calais. The sight of its walls and gate seemed to promise them food, shelter, and an exchange of booty for good gold, but to the dismay of the vast majority, only the Earl of Warwick's men were allowed to enter. Thomas Malory was one of these; he slept that night with a full stomach and a roof over his head. The others, such as Thomas Hostell, saw the gate shut against them. They were the real victors of Agincourt, but there was not enough food in the town to feed the extra thousands. They were told that the King had ordered large supplies of food to be sent from England; they must wait until the ships arrived. In the meantime, they bartered away the plunder they had carried so painfully from the battlefield until most were left as empty-handed as when they had come from home.

By October 29 Richard Beauchamp had returned from England to Calais. That day he learned that the King would be arriving immediately with his captives. He set out to meet them, leading a cavalcade of citizens, priests, and men of his own retinue. Thomas Malory had the honor of riding with Sir John Beauchamp to meet the King. He heard the chanting of praises to God and the shouts of loyal soldiers still camped outside the walls of Calais, waiting for transport home to England. Within the city, English banners flew from every window and cheers resounded in all the streets. But the King did not smile. Everyone noticed it and wondered at it.

A month later, those at Calais heard about the stupendous celebration which took place when on November 23 Henry finally reached London. The Lord Mayor, the clergy, and city officials, all in fur-trimmed scarlet gowns, made a procession with London craftsmen and merchants, fifteen thousand strong, riding as far as Greenwich to meet the returning conqueror. London Bridge was decorated with flags and banners, bells rang from every steeple, and fountains were filled with wine. To the sound of trumpets and drums the King rode into his city while choir boys dressed as angels sang:

> Our King went forth to Normandy
> With grace and might of chivalry;
> The God for him wrought marvelously
> Wherefore England may call, and cry
>   Deo gratias:
> Deo gratias Anglia redde pro victoria.

Guinevere

Thomas Malory heard that "Victory Song of Agincourt" sung by minstrels all the days of his life. Thanks be to God for Agincourt! Yet when the King, followed by his captives, had passed through the streets of London to celebrate his victory by hearing Mass at St. Paul's, those who saw him said that he never once smiled.

It was as if he alone understood what had happened and what was yet to come. Or so it seemed to Thomas Malory, remembering the King's face as he had seen it at Calais after the battle. For in spite of the overwhelming victory at Agincourt, France did not fall into Henry's hands. The Armagnac force under the Duke of Orléans had been cut to pieces, but the King of France and his son the Dauphin with all of their army were still untouched. No one knew as yet whether John the Fearless, the formidable Duke of Burgundy, would choose to support France or England. Only a few days after Henry's triumph in London, Charles VI and the Dauphin entered Paris to prevent the Duke of Burgundy from seizing the city himself. Burgundy could not be counted on either as an enemy or as a friend.

Meanwhile, the noble French captives were put into English prisons. Charles, Duke of Orléans, the most famous prisoner of Agincourt, was lodged, with respect, but under close bonds, in the Tower of London. Thomas Malory had never again seen him after the day when they both rode into Calais following King Henry. But he often thought of the Duke, who was to pass twenty-five years of captivity in England. He too had loved books and spent time writing in prison. Perhaps Charles of Orléans had used some book, French or English, for inspiration when he wrote his charming couplet:

> *All by myself, wrapped in my thoughts*
> *And building castles in Spain and in France.*

Everyone knew Master Geoffrey Chaucer's lines, translated from the French, and so similar:

> *Thou shalt make castles then in Spain,*
> *And dream of joy, all but in vain.*

Thomas Malory was expert in detecting such resemblances. He too was a gatherer of other men's flowers.

The Duke of Orléans had at last been released and allowed to return to France. There he wrote of his long purgatory: "I have had experience myself in English prisons, and for the weariness, danger, and displeasure in which I then lay I have many a time wished I had been slain at the battle where they took me." On this score, at least, Thomas Malory felt for a fellow prisoner, even a French one. He wondered whether the Duke was still in an English prison when he wrote the line so much admired in England:

> *Je meurs de soif en côté la fontaine.*

If the Duke had been an Englishman, like Thomas Malory, and in an English prison, one of the victors of Agincourt rather than one of the vanquished, how much more would he have felt that he was "dying of thirst by the side of the fountain"!

As for John, Duke of Bourbon, he had been imprisoned in Newgate until he was carried out dead twenty-five years later, to be buried in Greyfriars Church. Thomas Malory, thinking of his own death, wished to be buried there too if it could be arranged. It was said that even the greatest sinners were safe from the assaults of the devil if they were buried in Greyfriars Church, wrapped in the robe and cowl of a friar. Thomas Malory knew his own sins and knew that he had need of protection from hell's fire.

He continued to ponder on the life and death of kings. The irony was that King Henry's French captives had lived far longer than the King himself. With all their misery, they were safe in their English prisons while he had soon been forced to continue his war to the death in France.

True, there were still to be successful ventures, and in each of these times of triumph Richard Beauchamp was at the King's right hand. The year after Agincourt the Emperor Sigismund brought the famous heart of St. George in its golden reliquary to Calais. There Richard Beauchamp entertained Sigismund with such magnificence that the Emperor called him "the Father of Courtesy." Escorted by a fleet of three hundred ships, Sigismund then sailed for England, where he presented the holy relic of St. George to Henry and signed a treaty making the Holy Roman Empire the ally of England for all of Henry's French claims.

The signing of this treaty, on August 15, 1416, was a notable event, and the aim was still more glorious. With a united Europe the two powerful rulers would heal the schism in the Church; with a united Christendom they would then drive the Turkish infidels from the Holy Land. Sigismund spoke openly of his admiration for Richard Beauchamp as the diplomat who had influenced him to move toward the treaty with England.

The next move must be an alliance with the Duke of Burgundy. Richard Beauchamp returned to France and brought the Duke to Calais for a meeting with King Henry and the Emperor Sigismund. The private thoughts of the wily Duke were hard to fathom, but he seemed ready to cast his lot with Henry against the imbecile King of France and his Armagnac allies. France was sure to fall.

In the following year, one of King Henry's great objectives was achieved. Martin V was elected Pope of a united Church. Again King Henry and the Emperor Sigismund paid tribute to Richard Beauchamp's skill as a diplomat and his devotion as a son of the Church in bringing success to the council meetings at Constance. It seemed that everything he touched succeeded. To serve this man was happiness indeed, and Thomas Malory, now seventeen years of age, was happy.

But France did not fall; even Normandy did not surrender to King Henry. He prepared for a return to grim warfare. This time his plan was to divide Normandy into three parts, with his brother, the Duke of Clarence, and Richard Beauchamp as the other two leaders. As castles and fortresses fell, they would be given English commanders to collect taxes from the surrounding countryside. In this way the cost of the war would be paid by those who should pay, the French people, who through stubborn resistance were denying King Henry, their true king, his rights. Meanwhile, England paid for the war. At Newbold Revel, Sir John Malory, now sheriff for Warwickshire, was assessed the wages of a lance and two archers, who soon sailed to Calais with a detachment of other men from Warwick. But as sheriff Sir John was a richer man than he had been. He could afford to pay.

Once again, in the summer of 1417, a great fleet of ships was loaded with men and supplies. Once again news came to Calais that King Henry had landed at the mouth of the river Seine. A few miles to the south lay the strongly fortified city of Caen, his first objective. Both the Duke of Clarence and the Earl of Warwick came to their sovereign's aid for the attack on this great city. Among Richard Beauchamp's four hundred lances and bowmen were the three

Guinevere

sent by Sir John Malory; among Beauchamp's hundred men-at-arms was young Thomas Malory.

He had never seen a city as big as Caen. Its walls and towers, surrounded by deep water-filled moats, looked impregnable. This was William the Conqueror's city; he had laid the foundations for the castle within the walls, a fortress within a fortress. But King Henry's confidence and energy were equal to any challenge, and his men responded. Experienced now in reducing cities by siege and attack, the English army set up a vast camp on a hillside, while the King established headquarters outside Caen in the strong-walled abbey where William the Conqueror lay buried. In the shadow of the Conqueror's tomb Henry sat giving commands and dispensing justice.

He had brought from England an array of cannon and these he mounted on the abbey walls. A frightful bombardment began, while foot soldiers assembled a bridge, made of leather and brought from England. On this they crossed the moat. The French defenders of Caen fought back by pouring scalding water and boiling pitch and oil on those men who reached the walls. But the shattering blows of huge stone projectiles and the deafening noise of rock exploding against rock could not be withstood forever.

On September 4 the Earl of Warwick and the Duke of Clarence broke through the walls of Caen and their victorious men poured into the city. The castle surrendered. The red tide of battle surged over victims and victors alike. The attack became a bloody rout. At one moment an army of disciplined soldiers were occupying a city; at the next moment they were plunging through the streets in a blind fury. The dead were piled in heaps among the wreckage.

That day Thomas Malory saw Caen as if a mist of blood

had covered his eyes. His sword was red; his hands were red and filled with plunder. The English leaders were going through the streets shouting the King's commands against robbing any church or harming any women; at last, order was restored in the English army. Caen was rich. The English soldiers returned to their camp with enough booty to satisfy their wildest dreams, but no one forgot the berserk rage that had possessed them. The French did not forget.

The next day Richard Beauchamp knighted many squires. It was usual after a victory to reward valor; he knighted Thomas Malory. There was no vigil, no time for prayer, but the chosen squires went again into the city and entered the church of St. Peter. Thomas Malory knelt before his lord. He felt the light touch of the sword on his shoulder and heard Richard Beauchamp's voice saying the longed-for words, "Rise, Sir Thomas Malory." He looked into the serene and noble face. Then he looked higher. On the capital of a stone column he saw a carved figure. It was that of Launcelot crossing the sword bridge.

After Caen, city after city in Normandy fell to the English armies by siege or by assault, sometimes even without a fight. For his part, Richard Beauchamp took a number of the fortresses whose capture would bring Normandy to her knees and open the river Seine as a route to Paris. Rouen, "master city of Normandy," lay fifty miles up river from Harfleur, and to capture it would require the united strength of all the English soldiery.

While Richard Beauchamp was still attacking smaller cities, his men learned that the Duke of Burgundy had entered Paris, increasing his threat to the French throne, but

Guinevere

the crafty Duke was also assisting the Armagnac forces against Henry wherever possible. Rouen was in Burgundian hands. This was how matters stood at the end of July 1418, when Richard Beauchamp turned his men toward Rouen. They understood that Rouen would be a test of endurance to the end, but they were hardened, seasoned fighting men now, one and all, and they had no thought but victory.

Even before the arrival of the Earl of Warwick, English forces had sealed Rouen off from the possibility of French help. The river was blocked in both directions by barricades of ships and chains. Each of the city's gates was heavily guarded to prevent any movement into or out of the town. It was the beginning of a siege more difficult and damaging than any which Thomas Malory had yet seen.

Rouen had prepared for the siege by destroying every house and church that could provide shelter for the attackers, every garden and planted field that could give forage. Its walls and every one of its sixty towers bristled with guns and its deep moat was pitted with hidden traps.

There were spurts of violent action, but siege more than any other kind of warfare called for long days of waiting. The autumn passed and winter came. The King kept his English soldiers well supplied with good beef, bread, and ale. They ate and drank, they sat in their tents or around their campfires sleeping, talking, playing at dice. Some kept journals. Thomas Malory, stationed with Warwick's men at the Martinville gate to the east of the city, began to write at this time. Another English soldier, John Page, at a north gate, was writing about the siege of Rouen in a poem that was to make him famous. Like many others who witnessed the siege, he was not without feeling for the gallantry of Rouen's fighting men and the sufferings of its people.

John Page told how the King sent heralds into Rouen demanding its surrender. When the citizens did not deign to answer, the English guns opened a ferocious attack and the French responded with a brilliant sortie of armored knights on horseback who inflicted heavy losses on the English soldiers at the north gate.

Every day there was fighting at the north gate and at the south gate by the bridge over the river Seine. There was bitter fighting at the Martinville gate. Often thousands of men made sorties from all the gates of Rouen at the same time. "It must have been a great joy to lead them," wrote John Page in his poem, "but it was terrible to encounter them; not merely because of their bravery in defending themselves, but also because of the guns and cross-bows which were firing on us from the walls. I have never experienced such a thing before. The moment they made a sortie at least a hundred cannon would fire from the walls and towers for a whole hour, and no tongue can tell how many cross-bow shafts were loosed. Always the besieged were trying to break out, though many of them fell.

"News now arrived that the Duke of Burgundy was coming with 400,000 men to rescue the city and our king ordered that every man should sleep fully clothed and armed for battle. But the Burgundians did not come.

"Toward Christmas food became so scarce in the city that the people were eating dogs and cats, rats and mice. They even grubbed in the dirt for roots. Every day many in the city were dying. Mothers no longer shared a last bit of bread with starving children but hid it and ate it themselves in secret.

"One day the gates opened and all the poor, the old, and many women and children were forced out. Some had come from Harfleur three years before. We saw women with babies in their arms begging us on their knees for food. Old men knelt beside them wailing and crying for mercy. We could not let them pass our outposts. We gave them bread, but we had to make them go down into the moat and stay there.

"It was very cold and it was Christmastime. On Christmas Day our king sent food into Rouen, enough for all within the walls and also for the poor people outside. But after they had eaten, the fighting began again and the hunger began again. 'War has three handmaidens ever waiting on her,' said our king, 'Fire, Blood, and Famine, and I have chosen the meekest of the three.' "

Hunger breaches even walls of the hardest stone. On New Year's Day Rouen asked for a truce and long parleys were held. Richard Beauchamp headed the negotiations for the English side, meeting the French leaders in fine tents set up outside the city walls for the purpose. Thomas Malory had the honor of riding with Sir John Beauchamp to accompany his cousin the Earl of Warwick.

"It was a solemn sight for both sides to see," John Page wrote, "the splendid tents, the citizens crowded on the city walls, our soldiers parading and the brilliant heralds going from one tent to the other. Both English and French wore surcoats glittering with gold. But this was a bitter sight for the poor folk in the moat. They had but a few rags to cover their nakedness and protect them from the cold. Children of two or three years of age wandered about begging for bread. Some of these wretched people were unable to open their eyes, others cowered on their knees as thin as twigs. A woman was there clutching her dead child to her breast to warm it, and a child was sucking the breast of its dead mother."

On the eighth day the commander of Rouen surrendered the keys to the city. The English soldiers marched into Rouen and John Page told what they saw: "It was pitiable. Many of the people were mere skin and bones with hollow eyes and pinched noses. They could scarcely breathe or talk. Their skin was dull as lead, like the dead rather than the living. In every street were corpses and hundreds of citizens crying out for bread. For many days afterwards they died, quicker than the carts could carry them to burial."

After the entrance of his soldiers, King Henry rode into Rouen. Once again, his dress and his face were somber. Once again he went straight to prayer, this time in the great cathedral. John Page, turning his notes into verse, felt that he had failed to find words worthy of the King's dignity and glory:

> *He rode upon a brown steed,*
> *In black damask was he clad;*
> *A breast-plate of gold full bright*
> *About his neck hung down right.*
> *To the minster did he fare*
> *And from his horse dismounted there;*
> *His chaplain met him at the door*
> *And went before him all in fur*

And sang a response full glorious
"*Quis est magnus dominus?*"

The following year events played into Henry's hands. At the end of May 1419, he met and kissed the French Princess Catherine, so long a part of his plans for the union of France with England. She was tall, slender, smiling, and winsome. Henry fell deeply in love with her. He proceeded vigorously toward the signing of a final treaty that would bring an end to the "unlusty war," as his soldiers were beginning to call it.

But whatever might be settled with the French King and his daughter, Henry still had to reckon with the Dauphin and the Duke of Burgundy. That summer it was known that these two had finally agreed to join forces against the English. They were to meet south of Paris at Montereau on a bridge that crossed the Seine. Since neither side trusted the other, barricades had been built at both ends of the bridge, and Duke and Dauphin, each with ten armed knights, advanced to an enclosure in the center. What happened there was never known. Suddenly there were cries, men were running with drawn swords from the enclosure, and the Duke of Burgundy was found dead there. He had been murdered by a blow from an ax.

It was said later that "through the hole in the Duke's skull the English entered France." Although the Dauphin was only a boy of sixteen, he was blamed for the murder, and the new Duke of Burgundy, Philip, son of John the Fearless, could think of nothing but avenging his father's death by opposing the Dauphin in every way. Without fear of Burgundian trouble, Henry was now able to conclude the important Treaty of Troyes with the King of France.

That poor invalid would retain his title for life, but Henry would govern in fact and inherit the throne of France. Henry's heirs were to rule France after him. Meanwhile, the war would continue against all parts of France that did not submit to his control.

In May 1420, Henry rode to Troyes, a hundred miles southeast of Paris for the signing of the treaty. Richard Beauchamp had arranged the truce; he now arranged the marriage between Henry and Catherine, which would take place immediately after the signing of the treaty. This ceremony, so long expected, was performed with great magnificence at Troyes on June 2.

But there was no time for romantic idling; dauphinist fortresses had to be taken. During the first months of her marriage Catherine went wherever her husband went, and his soldiers were heartened by occasional glimpses of her. Catherine did not share the soldiers' hardships. Henry found the best of houses for her and sent English minstrels to play and sing for her every morning and evening.

Through the autumn Richard Beauchamp continued with his own military conquests in Normandy. At last, on December 1, King Henry was able to ride into Paris as regent of France and heir to the throne. King Charles VI of France rode at his side. To achieve this, Henry had fought for six hard years. Richard Beauchamp had been at his side every step of the way. He was at his side now.

As they rode through Paris, Henry's followers marveled at the beauty of the city. They saw that the prize was worth the fight. After a Mass in Notre Dame, they understood the King's spoken wish to rebuild Westminster Abbey. The Louvre, which he occupied with his Queen, was a finer palace than any in London, finer than Windsor. But Henry had neither time nor money for building. He ordered the coronation of Catherine, then a royal progress with her through England. During his long absences in France his ministers and his people had remained faithful to him and his cause. They deserved to see him with his beautiful French bride, the symbol of his victory.

Early in February 1421, Richard Beauchamp and his retinue returned to England with King Henry and Queen Catherine for her coronation in London. If the King's reception on English shores was joyous after Agincourt, this time it was tumultuous. At Dover, Thomas Malory saw noblemen wading into the water and carrying the King and the Queen to land. London outdid any welcome ever given to any sovereign. At the gates, fantastic giants and lions nodded and bowed to the royal pair. The buildings of the city were completely covered with decorations. Choruses of minstrels sang, the streets were strewn with green branches, and once again the fountains flowed freely with wine. On Sunday, February 23, Catherine was crowned in Westminster Abbey.

Paris might be a grander city than London, but to Thomas Malory no sights or sounds could equal the crowning of Queen Catherine, the procession of nobles, and his own good lord among the first, the clear high notes of the clarion, echoing in the Abbey, repeated from the walls of London town, while all the bells pealed and the people one and all shouted, "Long live the Queen!"

It was time now for the royal progress through the King's realm. Not only would his loyal subjects see his beautiful wife, but his courtiers, traveling with him, could suggest and receive contributions to the royal treasury, which was nearly empty as a result of the wars in France. Richard

Beauchamp begged the honor of a visit from the King and Queen at Warwick and set off at once with his entire retinue to prepare for their arrival.

It was Thomas Malory's first sight of home in six years of service under his lord. He had left Warwick as a squire, raw and untried; he was returning as a knight and a seasoned man-at-arms. His mother looked somewhat frail and worn, though overjoyed to see him. His father was prosperous and in good health. He had served twice as a Member of Parliament and hoped to serve again. He had put his various properties in order and made additions and improvements at Newbold Revel. But Thomas's room was unchanged, and the yew tree stood as always outside his window. In the morning its branches were veiled in fog when Thomas rose early to ride with his father.

In his son's mind Sir John was still Sir Tristram, "who every day would go ride a-hunting, for Sir Tristram was that time called the best huntsman of the world, and the noblest blower of an horn." Now they hunted together as man and man, and Thomas once again shared with his father a huntsman's joys as he had loved to do when he was a boy.

No one had described those joys better than the King's uncle Edward, Duke of York, when he wrote the little book called *The Master of Game*. "Hunters," he said, "live in this world more joyfully than any other men, for when the hunter riseth in the morning, and he sees a sweet and fair morn and clear weather and bright and he heareth the song of the small fowls, and when the sun is arisen, he shall see fresh dew upon the small twigs and grasses, that is great joy and liking to the hunter's heart." And when he returns home, "he shall doff his clothes, and his shoes, and his hose, and he shall wash his thighs and his legs, and peradventure all his body. And he shall order well his supper, with good meats, and good wine and ale."

All of these joys Thomas Malory now tasted again, thanking God that he had lived through the French wars and had come safely home. After his bath and his supper at night, he slept well in his own bed, dreamed of hunting, and woke again to see the yew tree standing eternal in the light of another Warwickshire hunting morning. The Duke of York slept well too, but he dreamed no more of hunting. He had died at Agincourt and his bones rested in English soil.

When the royal guests came at last with their cavalcade through the gateway of Warwick Castle, Thomas Malory was on duty and counted himself fortunate to be present at this high moment in the lives of both his sovereign and his lord. The lady Elizabeth, Countess of Warwick, was not well and could take little part in the festivities, but the Earl's young daughters were beautiful children and they were on display. They were graciously noticed and admired by the King and Queen. No one mentioned the fact that there was no son.

Among the castle battlements the Earl pointed out the tower known as Guy's Tower, and in honor of Guy of Warwick rode out to Guy's Cliff to show the King where the legendary warrior had passed his last days. Henry had known the story since youth. He walked thoughtfully through the shady woods by the sparkling stream, explored Guy's cave, and visited the hermit who in those days lived in a cottage beside a small chapel.

King Henry knelt in the chapel and prayed aloud for a son. The Earl too knelt in prayer. The King then said that he would someday build a chantry at Guy's Cliff where two priests would sing Mass daily for the benefit of the Earl and his wife in things spiritual and temporal so long as they lived and for the health of their souls and the souls of all their family and friends.

The good days of the royal progress ended with a shock. The King learned that on March 22 his brother Thomas, the Duke of Clarence, had been killed in an ambush by forces of the Dauphin at the town of Baugé in Anjou to the south of Normandy. Henry did not shorten his travels through England, but early in June, leaving the Queen at Windsor, he was on his way from Dover to Calais with four thousand men-at-arms. One thought consoled him: the Queen was expecting a child.

For Richard Beauchamp and a large retinue of his men, the fighting resumed. Once again Thomas Malory was on French soil. That summer there were heavy rains and intense heat. Disease and hunger, so long familiar to the men who had already fought in France, beset the fresh troops; morale was low. There was fighting along the Seine and all around Paris, with stiff resistance from the armies of the Dauphin.

In the autumn King Henry began the siege of Meaux on the river Marne, east of Paris. The French commander of Meaux was famous for hanging every Englishman he captured. Richard Beauchamp led his own men-at-arms to the aid of the English besiegers. A rumor was going through their camp that the King was ill with the bloody flux, but he was here, there, and everywhere, as always, directing operations, sleeping little at night. He even summoned the energy to invent a new military device, a tower mounted on barges to float down the Marne and fire cannon into the city from above the height of its walls. Early in December he was heartened by news that the Queen had borne a son at Windsor. But this could not alter the fact that his health was being broken by the unrelenting strain of leading an army through the warfare of that winter. When Meaux fell in May, the King appointed Richard Beauchamp to receive the keys of the city while he himself went to Paris to recover his health.

With the English army, Thomas Malory saw the surrender of Meaux and the hanging of its commander. As a follower of Sir John Beauchamp, he entered the city when the Earl of Warwick rode through its gates, and he heard the daily reports that came to the Earl from Paris.

King Henry had moved his court to the castle of the Bois de Vincennes, three miles from the center of the French capital. Now Queen Catherine was with him and they were to pass a splendid Whitsuntide at the Louvre. Charles VI and his Queen were also in Paris, but they were seldom seen and were left almost alone. The French King was now a hopeless invalid and could not live long. Soon afterward Queen Catherine went to her father.

Meanwhile, word came from the Duke of Burgundy that the forces of the Dauphin Charles were northeast of Paris, at Cosne. If the Dauphin took this city he could drive a wedge between Burgundy and Paris. Ever since the murder of his father, the new young Duke of Burgundy had been a strong and active ally of King Henry; Burgundy must have support. Early in July Richard Beauchamp was ordered to take an English army to the relief of Cosne. The King would meet him there with another large force and would lead the combined armies.

One more attack, one more siege. The heat of that summer was fiercer with every day that passed and the suffering of the army was acute. Smallpox had broken out among the French children and there were deaths from the disease among the English soldiery. Mutinous whispers swept through the army. Was this war to go on forever? They had come to win back Normandy for their King. Now it seemed that they were expected to take all of France, and the French, beaten here, rose up there. The English had to recapture cities which Englishmen had bled and died to take. This man had lost his best friend, that one his brother. A few did the unthinkable: they deserted.

Thomas Malory followed his lord to Cosne. He never forgot the terrible days there while rumors concerning the King passed through the army. The King was sick with the smallpox. No, he was much better. He had gone to the country to recover his strength and would soon take over the command at Cosne. But the King did not come. He sent his army under the command of his brothers, but he himself did not come.

With the arrival of the King's own men early in August, Thomas Malory learned the truth. King Henry had indeed set out for Cosne, on horseback. It was plain to everyone who saw him that he was in agony, but he had ridden for fifty miles. Then at a town on the Seine he had been forced to stop. A rest of two weeks seemed to restore him somewhat, and a barge carried him comfortably by water toward Paris, away from the fighting. Near the city he tried once more to mount his horse in order to return to the Bois de Vincennes with royal dignity, but after a few moments he was faint with pain. A horse litter was brought and the King was laid in it. On August 10 he reached the Bois de Vincennes.

The Earl of Warwick was to go as soon as possible

with the King's brothers. Fortunately, the Dauphin, threatened at Cosne by both Burgundy and England, gave up the siege of the city and the English commanders were soon able to go to the King's bedside. Thomas Malory watched them ride away. Their departure was hasty and without ceremony. Everyone knew that they were going to the King's deathbed.

Slowly now, the news came back from Vincennes to Cosne. King Henry lay in a high tower room of the castle at Vincennes. He knew that he was dying and he put his affairs in the hands of the men he trusted most. His brother John, the Duke of Bedford, was to be regent of France, governor of Normandy, and guardian of the King's infant son, whom he knew that he would never see. His younger brother, Humphrey, Duke of Gloucester, was less dependable, but he had shown himself to be a good soldier and had been a faithful regent in England during Henry's absence; he was to continue as regent but would be subject to the supreme command of the Duke of Bedford. Both were to maintain the friendship of the Duke of Burgundy.

One more matter demanded the King's best thought. This was the care and education of his son. Until he came of age, he must be tutored and guided by the wisest counselors, and to this grave responsibility King Henry called Richard Beauchamp as well as the Bishop of Winchester, the Duke of Bedford, and the Duke of Exeter, who was especially loyal and devoted to King Henry and the house of Lancaster.

On August 31 the King asked his doctors how long he had to live. Reluctantly they told him that he could not hope for more than two hours. To this he answered that it was the will of the Saviour and according to the condition of all human flesh. If, therefore, he had ruled wrongly in any way or had done anyone an injustice, he asked pardon. But he could not think of any wrong or injustice that he had done. His only regret was that he could not live to carry the Holy Cross on a crusade to Jerusalem.

"Fight on," said the King, "until you have won a just peace, and remember that I myself fought for justice, not for glory." Soon afterward he seemed to be tormented as if by accusers or by a devil who had come to drag him down to hell. He was heard to say, "Thou liest! I am going to the lord Jesus Christ."

A priest gave the King extreme unction and his face became peaceful. He kissed the crucifix. The priest, putting his ear close to the King's lips, heard him reciting the twenty-first psalm, a psalm of David, who also had been a mighty ruler: "The king shall joy in thy strength, O Lord . . . Thou hast given him his heart's desire . . . thy right hand shall find out those that hate thee. Thou shalt make them as a fiery oven in the time of thine anger . . . For they intended evil against thee . . . thou shalt make ready thine arrows upon thy strings against the face of them." The lips were still.

The following year, Thomas Malory's path again crossed that of his cousin Philip Chetwynd. Philip had been close to the King's person ever since he had left Warwick Castle as a squire. When the King died at Bois de Vincennes, Philip was there. He told Thomas what he had seen after the King's death.

The body was carried down the flights of stone steps that led from the tower room to a guard room below. There the royal corpse was solemnly dismembered and the pieces were boiled to separate the flesh from the bones. Both

Guinevere

flesh and bones were then embalmed and encased in a leaden casket which was carried to St. Denis, the traditional burial place of French kings. In the great church the casket lay in state until an effigy could be made. This figure, covered with boiled leather, "very lifelike," said Philip, was dressed in robes of state and wore a golden crown. It lay on the casket, the scepter in one hand, in the other the orb.

On September 15, the lordly casket, mounted on a funeral carriage and drawn by four great horses, began the long journey toward its final resting place. At Rouen, Queen Catherine joined the mourners in the castle, where the casket again lay in state. (Was it strange that she had not come to her husband in his last illness?) Calais, Dover, Canterbury, London Bridge—everywhere there were throngs of people along the road, standing silent or weeping. First came a hundred men on foot, carrying torches that burned day and night as the long procession passed slowly on its way, the casket sheltered by a silken canopy, surrounded by white-robed priests, and followed by the black-clothed mourners, nobles all, mounted and riding two by two.

For a king who had spent so much of his life on horseback, it was fitting that the horses which drew his bier had trappings to symbolize all that the name of Henry V meant. The first horse bore the arms of Edward the Confessor, England's first patron saint; the second the arms of both France and England; the third the arms of France alone. The fourth horse was caparisoned with the arms of King Arthur, three golden crowns upon a shield of azure.

Had Arthur come again in the person of Henry V? There was much in him to remind his people of the noble and invincible Arthur. And never more so than at the end of his life when so many had seen the barge in which the dying King was rowed down the river Seine. For the old stories told how Arthur, mortally wounded, was carried by Sir Bedivere to the water side.

> And when they were there, close by the bank floated a little barge with many fair ladies in it, and among them was a queen, and they all had their heads covered with black hoods. And they all wept and cried out when they saw King Arthur.
> "Now put me into that barge," said the king.
> And so he did softly, and three ladies received him with great mourning . . .

There were no fair ladies with King Henry. Only rough soldiers rowed him to his resting place.

The story continued:

> And anon they rowed from the land, and Sir Bedivere cried and said, "Ah, my lord Arthur, what shall become of me, now ye go from me and leave me here alone among my enemies?"
> "Comfort thyself," said the king, "and do as well as thou mayest, for ye can no longer trust in me. For I must go into the vale of Avalon to heal me of my grievous wound. And if thou hear nevermore of me, pray for my soul!"

Strange, thought Thomas Malory, how the ancient images had been repeated during those last days of King Henry's life. The same, yet not the same. And now he wrote something all his own, something that was in none of the old tales:

> Men say in many parts of England that King Arthur is not dead but taken by the will of our Lord Jesus into another place; and men say that he shall come again, and he shall win the Holy Cross. Yet I will not say that it shall be so, but rather I would say, here in this world he changed his life.

Guinevere

The old *Morte Arthur* told of Arthur's grave at Glastonbury. Thomas Malory had once seen that grave—if it was Arthur's—but that was in later years. He had gone many times to see King Henry's grave in Westminster Abbey.

Early in his life the King had chosen a place for it, as near as possible to the tomb of St. Edward the Confessor, the most sacred spot in the Abbey. King Henry had ordered a chantry to be built for his tomb, high above all the people, so that even those at a distance could see it and see the priests at the altar there. Looking up, one saw, as Thomas Malory remembered well, figures carved in stone, King Henry on a prancing charger, riding at full gallop toward a castle where corpses hung from the battlements. On a beam above the chapel hung the King's shield, his saddle, and his helmet. As time passed, people began to say that this was the helmet which King Henry had worn at Agincourt, but Thomas Malory knew that it was not so. He had reason to know.

Thomas Malory laid down his pen. He had finished his work and he thanked God that he could depart from this world in peace. For a while he sat looking at the manuscript leaves tied and stacked in piles on his table. Then he took up his pen again, dipped it into his inkwell, and wrote:

> Here is the end of the whole book of King Arthur and of his noble knights of the Round Table, that when they were all together there were an hundred and forty. And here is the end of the Death of Arthur.
>
> I pray you all, gentlemen and gentlewomen that read this book of Arthur and his knights from the beginning to the ending, pray for me while I am alive that God send me good deliverance. And when I am dead, I pray you all pray for my soul.

For this book was ended the ninth year of the reign of King Edward the Fourth, by Sir Thomas Malory, knight, as Jesu help him for his great might, as he is the servant of Jesu both day and night.

The ninth year of the reign of King Edward IV, the year of our Lord, 1470, and he, Thomas Malory, was alive to see the work finished. In spite of his racking cough, his aching bones, the chilblained fingers that throbbed with every move of his pen, and the weakness that overwhelmed him at times like a rising tide, he had finished the work. It was more and more of an effort to sit up. Now he could lie down as much as he liked. One day he would lie down for good and all.

He pulled his blanket around him, eased his back onto the narrow bed, and lay staring at the ceiling. The friars, Brother John or Brother James—whoever came today— would take away the last of his stories, the Death of Arthur, to make a copy and return his own manuscript to him. It was all there on his table, the whole book, complete. Too late to make many changes now, but if he ever found the strength to do it, he would like to look over his book once more. He had done well with the men, or so he believed. Certainly a reader would feel the truth of Arthur, and Launcelot, and Gareth, perhaps of Merlin and Gawain, of Tristram, and Mordred, and even Galahad.

But what of the women? It occurred to him that he had spent most of his life with men, in the fortress or on the battlefield. The ladies stayed at home with their embroidery, their music, their chaplets of flowers. They were the grace and ornament of life, but he had had little of that. Women remained a mystery to him, and perhaps he had written of them as mysteries. How fair they were! a lady rising from a lake with a sword in her hand, a faraway princess waving her hand from a high window, ladies appearing in a forest, healing wounds, weaving spells. Some were witches and wove evil spells or brewed deadly poisons.

Now that he thought of it, the ladies he had known in his own lifetime had become strangely powerful in many ways. They were often keen-witted behind their soft smiles. While their husbands were far away, they managed great households, collected libraries, subtly changed the atmosphere of castle life. He had noticed it each time when he returned from the wars. To please the ladies during their long evenings alone, minstrels sang less of war and knightly combats, more of love and intrigue. Women without husbands for years at a time often took lovers.

In his own mind there was a puzzle, never resolved. The old stories told of Queen Guinevere's love for Launcelot. She was his lady; he was her devoted knight. But was she nonetheless faithful to King Arthur? The tales told it both ways and he had told it both ways. He had written:

> As the French book saith, the queen and Sir Launcelot were together. And whether they were abed or at other manner of amusement, I cannot say, for love then was not as love is nowadays.

And again,

> Perhaps my lady the Queen sent for him so that Sir Launcelot should come privately to her to avoid scandal; for oftentimes we do many things that we think are for the best, and yet it may turn out for the worst.

To the very end Launcelot was defending the Queen against all the evil that was said of her and swearing to King Arthur that his wife was "both true and good."

Ah well, the ladies would like it left a puzzle, as they themselves were puzzles. Faithful or not, Queen Guinevere's love for Launcelot had been a scandal at Arthur's court and had brought about the whole ruin of the Round Table. But out of the wreckage still shone the enduring names of Arthur and Guinevere as king and queen, of Launcelot and Guinevere as true lovers.

As for Queen Catherine, what could he believe of her? Why did she not come to her husband when he was dying at the castle of Vincennes? True, her own father was even then dying; he had died soon after King Henry. Had she chosen to stay with her old mad father? The puzzle remained.

And after King Henry's death, how soon she had taken a lover! She could not marry again without the consent of Parliament and she had defied them all by giving herself to a young Welshman, Owen Tudor, a mere squire, with whom she lived, and whom she finally married, bearing child after child, to the dismay of all who honored the memory of the King. The name of Tudor amounted to nothing in affairs of state. Strange that she who had been a queen should openly choose the folly of such a love match.

Catherine had lived on for fifteen years after the death of King Henry. In 1436 Owen Tudor was sent to prison in Newgate. The next year Catherine died—in an abbey to which she retired, as Guinevere had retired in her last sad days. No one had known what to do with her body, which must not be dishonored but which could not receive honor. She was embalmed, plainly clothed, and put into a plain rough coffin, open to public view. There she lay, in a chapel of Westminster Abbey, year after year, where she could be seen and even touched by any common person.

Guinevere

For all Thomas Malory knew, she was there still, as beautiful as ever. She was a mystery. The world had seen her at the King's side, royally dressed, smiling her winsome smile, and all the while her mind was busy with private thoughts. Her fatal beauty had wrecked the Lancastrian dynasty. It all came about through the innocent child whom she had borne to her husband, King Henry V, the child who was to be King Henry VI.

GALAHAD

"And anon the old knight led him to the Siege Perilous where beside sat Sir Launcelot, and the good man lifted up the cloth and found there the letters that said thus: THIS IS THE SIEGE OF SIR GALAHAD THE HIGH PRINCE . . . *Then all the Knights of the Round Table marveled greatly of Sir Galahad that he dared sit there and was so tender of age."*
                                                    THE QUEST OF THE HOLY GRAIL

THOMAS MALORY looked back on 1422 as a year when the world trembled and changed. It was the year when the death of Henry V left a baby as heir to the crowns of England and France. It was the year when the death of the French King, Charles VI, left a weak and foolish Dauphin with no crown to call his own. It was the year when Richard Beauchamp's first wife, Elizabeth, died at Warwick, leaving him no son.

He must have a son. Soon after the death of his Countess, he chose a second wife, the lady Isabella Despencer, the young widow of his cousin (another Richard Beauchamp) the Earl of Worcester, who had been killed in the fighting at Meaux. Her new husband then set about founding a chantry at Guy's Cliff, as Henry V had wished to be done. Thomas Malory wrote of it as "that hermitage which was under a wood, and a great cliff on the other side, and a fair water running under it." Richard Beauchamp ordered the building of a chapel at Guy's Cliff with a great statue of Guy of Warwick, nine feet high, carved in one of its stone walls. He paid for two priests to live there and to pray for the birth of his son.

At court he took fatherly care of the infant King, as Henry V had charged him to do. It was a grave responsibility, for under the guidance of "the Father of Courtesy" the child was expected to grow up as a perfect knight and perfect king.

The Earl of Warwick was still carrying the baby King in his arms in public processions and other ceremonies, even meetings of Parliament, when his own son was born. He named his child Henry.

It was soon noticed that the two children were alike not only in name. Both were fair-haired, gentle, and amiable. Both seemed to have a natural love for all the rites of the Church, an understanding of holy things, and a sincere desire to grow in grace. As Thomas Malory remembered them, they were like the two Galahads of the old tales. One was Galahad, the son of Launcelot; the other was Galahad, "the high prince." He had put both Galahads into his own tales, and those who wished could see the likeness to Henry Beauchamp, son of "the best knight of the world" and to Henry VI, the high prince of the house of Lancaster.

During the early childhood of the two boys, Richard Beauchamp's duties as a father and a foster father were

Galahad

easy, but his other burdens were becoming heavier. Humphrey, Duke of Gloucester, Protector and Defender on behalf of the little King, was a restless and unreliable man. He now threw himself into a love affair with a married lady. Her name was Jacqueline, Countess of Hainaut and Holland, and she had inherited rich lands which the Duke of Burgundy needed. He, already chafing under his alliance with England, fiercely resented the so-called marriage to the Duke of Gloucester. It took all the tact and judgment of responsible leaders like Richard Beauchamp to avoid a total break between England and Burgundy.

Meanwhile, the kingliness of Henry VI had to be shown to his people as soon as possible. In 1426, when he was only five years old, his uncle John, Duke of Bedford, interrupted military campaigns against the Dauphin in France to knight the young child at Leicester. Thomas Malory's father, Sir John, had relatives and property near Leicester. He made the day's ride with his family and retainers from Newbold Revel to see and be seen when the great lords were gathering. It was an occasion that touched all hearts. Thomas Malory, now in Richard Beauchamp's own retinue, was present when the little King, looking like a young angel, bowed his fair head and knelt to receive the touch of the sword on his shoulder.

In spite of the old saying that there was woe in the land when a child was king, young Henry's guardians moved rapidly toward his crowning. A king crowned and anointed with holy oil was sacred and therefore safe from harm by any but the most villainous of traitors.

Thomas Malory remembered well the November day in 1429 when the coronation of the child King took place in Westminster Abbey. He saw again the loved figure of

Richard Beauchamp guiding the little boy in each movement of the elaborate solemnities, while the highest lords and ladies of the realm barely restrained their tears. Could the small head and hands of this angelic child bear the weight of the crown, the scepter, and the orb?

The light of candles and torches shone on his gentle face as he sat enthroned where his great father had sat, but to Thomas Malory, remembering it from the shadows of his prison, Henry VI seemed all of his life to have been surrounded by shadows. The first shadow was cast by his mother, the beautiful Catherine of Valois, through whom he inherited the insanity of his grandfather, Charles VI.

The second shadow was already looming when he was crowned King of England. It appeared in the shape of a girl, mounted on horseback and riding through France followed by a victorious French army. She said that she had visions of saints and heard their voices telling her to save France.

Her name was Joan of Arc and she came from Domrémy, a village of Lorraine. She wore a soldier's armor and lived like a soldier, but they called her "the Maid" in token of her virgin purity. She carried a banner emblazoned with lilies. For her sake the soldiers of her army honored the chastity of their countrywomen as no soldiers had ever done before. She reminded them that English soldiers sprinkled their talk with "goddamns"; French soldiers should be better men than the English. They stopped swearing and even, though reluctantly, gave up looting. Led by the Maid with her lily banner, they were recapturing town after town that English armies had bled and died to take. Their battle cry was "For God and the Maid!"

The English captains called her "the French whore" and

it was very clear to the Duke of Bedford that she was from the devil, not from God. She had evidently put a spell on the Earl of Suffolk, who seemed unable to mount an offensive against her. There were all sorts of legends about her. One said that Merlin, the enchanter, had foretold the coming of a maid from Lorraine who would rise from a magic wood near Domrémy to save France. Another story claimed that wounded soldiers were healed if they so much as touched her garments. She said that they would find a sword for her behind the altar of a church where she stopped to pray, and the sword was found where she had said it would be. When the priest at that church touched it, the rust fell away and the sword blazed as if with fire—a magic sword.

In March the Maid had gone to Chinon to find the Dauphin. When she entered the castle, a man-at-arms called out with an oath what he would do if he could have her for a night. "In the name of God," she said to him, "do you dare to blaspheme when you are so near your death?" That night the man was drowned in the castle moat. Certainly she was a witch.

At Chinon she recognized the Dauphin, whom she had never seen before, and said, "Most noble lord Dauphin, I am Joan the Maid, sent by God to aid you and your kingdom, and He orders me to tell you that you will be crowned in the city of Rheims."

In May she had entered Orléans while a besieging army of English soldiers stood as if frozen by an evil spell. Once, wounded in battle herself, she plucked out the arrow and returned to the fight. She fell from a scaling ladder but was unhurt. Only witches could do such things.

In July she led the Dauphin through country held by the

English to Rheims, the ancient city where kings of France were crowned. When the crown was put on his head, the Maid stood beside him with her lily banner.

But the wearing of a crown could not put wisdom into the head of the new King Charles VII, or fidelity into his heart. It was soon known that on the very day of his crowning he received an embassy from the Duke of Burgundy and offered to give Paris and most of northern France in exchange for the Duke's support. Seizing the opportunity, the Duke of Bedford moved quickly to strengthen England's hand. He brought in English soldiers to help Burgundy reinforce Paris and he reminded the Duke how dauphinist traitors had murdered the Duke's father on the bridge at Montereau. He pointed out that Charles was allowing ignorant peasants to join the forces of "a disorderly woman in men's clothing." All England remembered the bloodbath that had followed the rising of John Ball and of Wat Tyler. If the passions of the peasants got out of hand, no one could foretell the end of the trouble.

Indeed, the Duke of Burgundy understood this danger. He knew that the common people were talking less of Charles's party or the Burgundian party; instead they talked of "France." By this they seemed to mean the land itself, the land on which they humbly labored. They talked as if the land belonged to them and as if Joan, not Charles VII or the Duke of Burgundy, were their true leader. Besides, she who had begun her leadership as an obedient daughter of the Church continually talked of voices and visions that came to her, a peasant girl, not through the Church, but through God's saints from the Almighty Himself. Because of her, all the proper channels of power in France were being diverted.

Galahad

In England too there was chaos. Without the leadership of a strong king, Parliament broke out into violence. Sir John Malory was a Member of Parliament for Warwickshire at this time. He told his son, Thomas, what it was like to sit in fear of a riot in the very chambers of government. The Members of Parliament were forbidden to bring weapons to their meetings; instead they brought cudgels. When this too was forbidden, they came with stones and lumps of lead in their pockets.

It was time for a show of strength from the highest leadership existing in those dark days. In the spring of 1430 Richard Beauchamp took England's child King to France to crown him at Paris as soon as might be. Thomas Malory went with his lord. Philip Chetwynd went in close attendance to the person of the King.

Their arrival at Calais took place on April 23, the day of England's patron, St. George. As soon as young Henry set foot on French soil, he was mounted on a richly caparisoned pony and was led to the church of St. Nicholas to give thanks and to hear Mass. It wall part of a careful plan to remind the people that the new King's great father, Henry V, would have done the same.

Although Richard Beauchamp's recent duties had kept him mostly in England at this time, he was also Captain of Rouen. He now led his cavalcade to Rouen, where the child would be safe under his personal care until the proper time for his crowning in Paris.

Thomas Malory remembered Rouen as he had seen it in the days of the long siege ten years before when Henry V's armies had brought the proud city to its knees, when refugees lay starving in the moat and the victorious English found only living skeletons within the walls. Now Rouen was an English stronghold, well governed and prosperous. It was defended by both English and Burgundian troops. Thomas Malory's duties were in the castle with his lord, Richard Beauchamp, free of physical danger and even enjoying luxuries that were provided for the young King and his entourage. Serenely the child played at his games and studied his lessons. But the English lords around him were anxious and gloomy as reports of the Maid's continued victories reached Rouen. A month passed. Then, late in May, came wonderful news.

The Maid had entered Compiègne, a town fifty miles north of Paris and held by forces loyal to Charles. But there were rumors that her magic sword had disappeared. On May 23 she led an attack, riding out of Compiègne, over the drawbridge, wearing a red cloak and carrying her banner. She and her men surprised a small outpost of Burgundian soldiers. At first, victory seemed in her hands. But the noise of the fighting reached John of Luxemburg, who came with reinforcements for the Burgundians. Joan's troops decided that retreat was best. They ran back into the town, and the drawbridge was raised while she herself was still trying to rally them. Left with only a handful of followers, and conspicuous with her red cloak and banner, she was easily captured and was handed over to John of Luxemburg, who passed her on to the Duke of Burgundy.

With Joan in captivity, a new spirit swept the English troops and their fortunes changed. They began to win again. All that had been lost might yet be regained if someone could be persuaded to do away with the witch, once and for all. Compiègne was in the diocese of the Bishop of Beauvais, Pierre Cauchon, who wanted to be Archbishop of Rouen. Thomas Malory remembered Cauchon as a man of intellect, a doctor of the University of Paris, whose opinions and principles commanded grudging respect from both English and French. He was a member of the French Council surrounding the little King Henry VI at Rouen. Now the Duke of Bedford consulted him about bringing a charge of witchcraft against the Maid.

Cauchon thought that a charge of heresy was more likely to succeed, and was justified. For example, when one of Joan's fanatic followers, the Count of Armagnac, had asked her who was the true Pope, she answered that she would talk to her saints about it and let the Count know. Such blasphemous arrogance must be put down, and quickly. If she was found guilty of heresy, she would be executed; if not, the English could still keep her and do as they liked.

They were bringing her to Rouen, secretly and with stops along the way whenever the route to Rouen needed to be cleared of interference from her friends. It would be months before she arrived, and these months could be used to collect the needed facts.

The search began at Domrémy, where agents of the law found a certain tree in the dark woods above the village. The villagers believed that fairies danced there. They admitted that Joan as a child had gone there to dance with other children. They called it the Ladies' Tree. There was a village spring too where sick people came to drink. They left bits of rag on bushes near the tree and the spring. Left for whom? The fairies? The devil? Anyone could feel the air of witchcraft about the place. It was only a start, but it was the kind of evidence needed by the prosecution.

Richard Beauchamp gave orders in the name of King Henry VI for a full review of the troops in Rouen to prevent disturbances on the arrival of the witch. Late in December she came. Thomas Malory saw her for the first time riding on horseback through the castle gate, heavily guarded by men-at-arms on all sides. Her face was pale under a woolen cap. Her dark hair was cut as short as a soldier's and she sat like a soldier in her saddle, wearing a black leather jacket over a tunic of dark wool. At first glance it was hard to believe that she was a woman. High boots over long stockings fitted her legs, which were chained together beneath the horse. Her hands were chained behind her, a soldier leading the horse by the bridle. The courtyard of the castle was full of men watching as her leg chains were unfastened long enough for her to walk to a cell in a tower of the castle. Three jailers went in after her and the heavy door was locked and bolted. Two more soldiers stood guard outside.

Later Thomas Malory saw the Maid in her cell when he went there with Richard Beauchamp on a tour of inspection. She was sitting on a cot but rose when they entered and stood straight, looking boldly from one to the other. Her legs were shackled and the chains were attached to an iron staple driven into a thick beam.

To Richard Beauchamp's courteous questions she answered in a voice that was deep and ringing, never to be forgotten by anyone who heard it: "I protest against being kept in chains and irons." He reminded her that at Beaurevoir on the journey to Rouen she had been treated kindly and had repaid that kindness by attempted suicide, leaping sixty feet down from the top of a prison tower. She replied, "It is true that I have wished, and that I still wish, what any captive wants—to escape." Even now, forty years later, Thomas Malory could hear her voice speaking those words. He too had been a captive in many prisons. He had always tried to escape.

In spite of the chains, the Maid was soon sending a defiant message to John of Luxemburg: "I know well that these English will do me to death, thinking that after I am dead they will win the kingdom of France. But if the goddamns were a hundred thousand more than they are now, they shall not have the kingdom."

She said much the same thing to the Earl of Stafford when he went to see her in her cell. The Earl, a violent man, drew his sword and would have killed her on the spot except that Richard Beauchamp stepped between them and forbade Stafford to touch her. The Maid must be tried, not murdered. Every one of her followers, down to the humblest, must understand her guilt and desert her cause as Charles of France had evidently done already. He sent no offer of ransom, not even a message. In time her very memory would disappear and France would accept its rightful king, Henry VI, who was even now waiting to be crowned.

Richard Beauchamp did everything in his power to protect his prisoner. One day he heard her cry out and ran to her prison. When she told him that two of her guards had tried to rape her, he dismissed the men, punished them, and replaced them with others under the strictest orders not to molest her. The Duchess of Bedford was sent to examine her and reported that Joan was indeed a virgin.

She said that she wore men's clothing by God's command and for her own protection. Immediately a letter in the name of "Henry, by the grace of God, King of France and England" accused Joan of "leaving off the dress and clothing of the feminine sex, a thing contrary to divine law and abominable before God, and forbidden by all laws." This much was fact, beyond a doubt, and her judges could make much of it in her trial. The other accusations were more serious. They remained to be proven, but a net of evidence was closing around the Maid.

In February 1431, in the royal chapel of the castle of Rouen, the trial began. It was important that all things should be done correctly, and, looking back on it, Thomas Malory believed that it had been a fair trial. For example, Pierre Cauchon said publicly that it was his duty to seek the Maid's salvation rather than her death. And when she fell ill during Lent through eating some spoiled fish, Richard Beauchamp sent his own doctor to bleed her.

The Earl did not need to attend the long and tiring trial. Every word was recorded and he read each day's testimony in the suite of rooms where he did the King's work. In the end there was no lack of evidence and no way to save her life. She was condemned out of her own mouth.

She told the court that her voices came to her every day and that they came from God. She said to the Bishop, "You say you are my judge. Consider well what you do, for in truth *I* am sent from God and you are putting yourself in great peril." At this, a murmur ran through the courtroom, then silence as the clerks recorded the shocking words.

She was charged with vanity and hypocrisy in allowing her clothing to be touched as if it had healing power. She said that she had allowed it as little as possible, but the court was unimpressed. She was accused of taking upon herself the power which only the Church had to name a Pope. She repeated that her voices came from God. Every day she was sealing her own doom.

Sometimes her boldness made the spectators smile behind their hands. When she was asked, "In what form was St. Michael when he appeared to you?" she said, "I know nothing of his garments."

"Was he naked?"

She answered, "Do you think God cannot afford to clothe him?"

Her judges looked confused. It did not help her case.

And yet there were times when her answers had to be admired. She was asked whether she believed herself to be in a state of grace, and she answered, "If I am not, may God put me there; if I am, may He keep me there." When questioned about the Ladies' Tree and the magic spring at Domrémy, she said that she had never seen fairies there and put no faith in the old stories that a maid would come from the woods of Domrémy to perform miracles. From all sides, again and again, month after month, her judges questioned her about her visions, about her clothing, her sword, and her battles against the English. Month after month she answered so clearly and bravely that many in the court were swept with waves of sympathy. One of the English lords was heard to say under his breath, "By God, a glorious woman! She should have been born English." Later he denied saying it, but Thomas Malory remembered.

May came, the month for love and joy. Joan had fasted during Lent and after that had been ill again. Everyone saw that she was thin and frail as she was led to trial and returned to her cell. Clearly she was tiring, yet she seemed not to understand what could happen if she persisted in defying the court. She constantly made distinctions between the Church Militant on earth and the Church Triumphant in heaven. She said that she had only one judge, God. They asked her whether she had a command from her voices not to submit herself to the Church Militant and its judgments.

"What I answer is not whatever comes into my head," she told them. "What I answer is at their command. They do not command me not to obey the Church, but first our Lord must be served."

In the face of this quibbling it was decided after much deliberation to show her the instruments of torture which waited for those too hardened to submit to reason. The dungeon of the castle at Rouen was in a high round tower not far from Joan's cell. A crowd of men watched as she was taken there to meet her judges. They watched as she was led back to her cell, weeping.

Thomas Malory was one of many who pressed through the open door of the dungeon to see what she had seen. It was as if he looked at last beyond the dungeon of Warwick Castle into the torture chamber which he had not dared to look at as a boy. He saw now the rack on which a body could be laid and stretched until the bones were pulled from their sockets. He saw the thumbscrew. He saw the pipes for the ordeal by water, the irons for the ordeal by fire. The old question returned to haunt him. Had his good lord, Richard Beauchamp, Earl of Warwick, the best knight of the world, ever seen these things? Had he ordered their use? One thing was certain, thought Thomas Malory, a man could not let his mind dwell on torture and at the same time continue to carry out his duties.

He supposed that each man who saw the instruments of torture at Rouen must have wondered what he would say and do if he were threatened as the Maid was threatened. What had she said? "If you were to have me torn limb from limb and part my soul from my body, I would say nothing but what I have said. And if I did say anything else, afterward I should always say that you had made me say it by force." Thomas Malory asked himself if he could have done as well.

Galahad

It was now the twenty-third of May. Already in the old market square of Rouen a stake and pyre of wood waited, and still the Maid stood her ground. Since force had failed, perhaps kindness would move her. A young priest spoke to her gently: "Joan, my dear child, your trial is almost over. Do not separate yourself from our Lord Jesus Christ. You have believed in your visions and voices too easily. Young and simple as you are, you should listen to those who are wiser than you in godly learning. Think, if a soldier said, 'I will not obey the King or his officers,' would you not condemn him? Then what can you say of yourself?"

She was shaken by the young priest's argument, but she answered, "If I were at the place of execution, and I saw the fire lighted, and the executioner ready to build it up, and if I were in the fire, even so I would say nothing else but what I have said at this trial . . . I have nothing more to say."

Yet after all, there was more to say. During that night she must have thought again of the fire and herself in the midst of it. The next day the Bishop of Beauvais hurried into the apartments of the Earl of Warwick with a paper signed that morning by Joan at the abbey church of St. Ouen: "I, Joan, called the Maid, a miserable sinner, recognize the snare of error in which I was held. I have returned to our Mother Holy Church, confessing that I have grievously sinned in falsely pretending that I have had revelations from God and His angels. And all my words and deeds which are contrary to the Church I do revoke . . ." Since she did not know A from B, she had signed the paper with a cross.

Thomas Malory saw his lord start up from his chair. "Do you mean that she will escape us after all?" he asked.

"Never fear, my lord," answered the Bishop, and left the room. During the same day the Maid learned from his own lips what was to happen. "That you may make penance for your sins, we condemn you to prison for life, to eat the bread of sorrow and drink the water of affliction." That night the Bishop returned. He told the Earl that he had gone to see Joan in her cell. She was now wearing the robe of a penitent. Her head had been shaved. No one would guess that she was the same person who had ridden into the castle of Rouen six months before.

Three nights passed. On the morning of May 28 Richard Beauchamp was called to the prison to see for himself what had happened. He signaled that others should go with him as witnesses. Thomas Malory was one of them. They found the Maid wearing the male clothing that she had put aside. Her robe of penitence lay in a heap on the floor. She said that she had not promised to wear it forever and that she needed men's dress since one of the English lords—she did not know who he was—had tried to violate her. Besides, her voices had returned, telling her that she had done wrong to sign a confession in order to save her life. She had done this only for fear of the fire, and now she would rather die than live the rest of her life in prison.

The following day the Bishop of Beauvais formally reported to the other learned doctors and clergy the relapse of the witch and heretic. The Church would not carry out the death sentence; she was turned over to the English, the secular arm of government, to be burned at the stake.

On May 30 at eight o'clock in the morning the old market square of Rouen was filled. The Earl of Warwick had ordered his lieutenant, next in command after himself, to form a guard large enough to keep order and control the

Galahad

crowd. A thousand soldiers, both mounted and on foot, surrounded the tall stake and the bundles of wood heaped about it. Richard Beauchamp was not present but some of his knights were there to represent him. This was the memory that Thomas Malory dreaded most of all. It brought nightmares so horrible that he heard himself screaming as he woke from them.

In his dreams he was once again in the market square of Rouen, armed and on horseback. The Bishop of Beauvais appeared and mounted a platform with other judges. Thomas Malory heard the wheels of a wooden cart rumbling over the cobblestones and saw Joan, dressed in her penitent's robe, her arms bound before her. Now she was climbing the steps of the platform and facing her judges. The Bishop of Beauvais read a sermon to her as she stood with bowed head. At times the Bishop hurried his words and his voice sank so that the meaning was lost, but he took care to raise his voice so that all could hear the necessary final words: ". . . errors and crimes of schism, idolatry, invocation of devils . . . excommunication . . . hand you over to secular justice . . ."

She was left alone upon the platform. A sound, half shout, half moan, came from the crowd. The guard stirred uneasily. Some knights drew their swords. Then the English bailiff of Rouen ran up the steps of the platform. He gave an order. Soldiers surrounded the Maid and led her to the pyre. They bound her to the stake and put a tall paper cap on her head. The crowd laughed. Thomas Malory heard her sobbing like a child and calling out for help. He saw tears running down her face. In his dreams he leaped to her side with the sword which he had sworn to use in aid of the weak and helpless, and in fact on that May day of

1431 his hand had tightened on the pommel of his sword. But he had sat motionless in his saddle.

The laughter of the crowd died away. An English soldier near the pyre made a cross by tying two sticks together. A Frenchman put the cross into her hands. Already the fire was lit. The military guard felt the searing heat.

Suddenly a young French priest ran from a church, carrying a cross. He broke through the ranks of soldiers and stepped into the fire, holding the cross high. For a moment the stifling smoke drifted aside and Thomas Malory saw the Maid looking upward. The paper cap had burned away and her robe was in flames. The priest retreated a step at a time, his face distorted with horror. He looked wildly about and called to the crowd in a broken voice, "She told me to save myself."

Above the roar of the savage fire a voice cried out—was it in torment or in triumph?—"Jesus! Jesus!" One by one the crowd were falling to their knees. An English voice muttered, "We are lost. We have burned a saint."

When the fire died down, the ashes and charred remains of her body were thrown into the Seine. But a story rose among the French that her heart would not burn. Whether true or not, this and other stories kept her alive. She had once said, "As to God's love or hate for the English, and what he will do to their souls, I know nothing. But I do know that they will be driven out of France, except those that die here, and that God will send the French victory over the English." After her death French victories continued as if she once again led her soldiers.

Nevertheless, Richard Beauchamp redoubled his efforts to hold the land won by the spilled blood of so many Englishmen. Even while the fighting went on, he sent for his wife and child to join him at Rouen and he named the

Galahad

seven-year-old boy as leader of a military expedition against the French. They would see that a new generation of English was ready to carry on the war which had now been fought for almost a hundred years. It was a charming sight when little Henry Beauchamp rode his pony up and down the courtyard of Rouen's castle and waved his cap to the cheers of the soldiers. He played at games with his young King and happily tried on the velvets and furs that he would wear at the coronation, planned for December.

But the crowning of Henry VI in Paris was not the success it was meant to be. There was fear of violence from partisans of the Maid or of Charles, whom many Frenchmen still saw as their true king because the Maid had crowned him. They said that Rheims was the city where French kings should be crowned, not Paris. There was deep resentment that an English cardinal, Beaufort, great-uncle of English Henry, was to put the crown on his head, conducting the ceremony according to the English custom. And the French people remembered that Beaufort had been at Rouen and was instrumental in the death of Joan of Arc.

Few French people lined the streets to watch when Henry VI, closely guarded, a canopy barely sheltering his head from the winter weather, walked from the palace of the Duke of Bedford to the cathedral of Notre Dame. Most of those in the church were English and their spirits were low. At long last they saw what the great Henry V had fought and died to win: his son sat on the throne of France. But it was indeed a perilous seat. For this, how many had given their lives; kings, princes, dukes, and countless thousands of men unknown to fame. For this the Duke of Bedford was even now wearing his life away. For this the Earl of Warwick, "the Father of Courtesy," had taken on himself responsibility for the death of a girl whom some already were calling a saint. The full consequences of her death could not yet be seen.

And how had all these things come to pass? Staring into the darkness of his cell after a nightmare, Thomas Malory often went over the events which had led to the crowning of Henry VI as King of France. Those events, it seemed to him, went back and back as far as the mind of man could recall, as far back as the days of William the Conqueror and even earlier, all because two lands faced each other across narrow seas.

As for the matter of the Maid of Lorraine, Richard Beauchamp remained guiltless in the eyes of Thomas Malory. The Earl of Warwick had gone to France in the honorable service of his lord and king, Henry V. He returned there in the service of Henry VI. Worn out by the struggle, he died there, in Rouen, where the Maid had died. Because of her death he died.

Could Richard Beauchamp have saved her? If she had been a queen, a lady, a gentlewoman, he might have gone to her aid as his ancestor Guy of Warwick, traveling through Normandy, had gone to the rescue of a high-born maiden about to be burned at the stake. The old tales also told how when Queen Guinevere was accused of treason, Sir Gawain refused to bring her to the stake or to witness the judgment against her. In the same story, Sir Gaheris and Sir Gareth said to King Arthur,

> "Sir, you may command us to be there, but it is sore against our will. If by your strict commandment we go, you must hold us guiltless, for we will be there unarmed." . . . And so the queen was led forth and undressed down to her shift. And her

Galahad

confessor was brought to her so that she might be forgiven for her misdeeds. And there was one that Sir Launcelot had sent to that place to espy what time the queen should go to her death. And anon as he saw the queen undressed down to her shift, and shriven, he gave Sir Launcelot warning.

And Thomas Malory wrote, his pen racing over the paper, how Sir Launcelot came with his friends to rescue the Queen. They fought their way through the crowd, killing many good knights, even Sir Gaheris and Sir Gareth, unarmed as they were.

And Sir Launcelot rode straight to Queen Guinevere as she stood ready for the fire, and ordered a kirtle and a gown to be put upon her and took her up behind him and rode away with her to Joyous Gard. And there he kept her as a noble knight should do.

Sir Tristram had done a nobler deed. He forgave a wicked queen, his stepmother, who had plotted his death by poison. When she stood bound at the stake, he begged for her life and "went to the fire and with the consent of the king delivered her from death." But Tristram and the queen were forever banished from the court of that king. He himself would have been banished, thought Thomas Malory, if on that May day at Rouen he had drawn his sword, spurred his horse, and, taking the Maid behind him, had fought his way to safety for her.

She could have disappeared into the countryside, hidden by her friends, and lived out her life in some quiet village, but he would have lost his good lord, his King, his native land. And all for what? a witch? a French whore?

No, she was not that. He knew now, and had known since the day when he saw her die, that she was what she claimed to be, Joan, the Maid, the virgin. Suddenly, flooding out of the past came an old song,

> *I sing of a maiden
> That is matchless* . . .

Then, as loud and clear as the voices that had come to her from heaven, he heard the voice of the Maid herself: "Consider well what you do, for in truth I am sent from God." Then the echo of an English voice: "We are lost. We have burned a saint." And another, "By God, a glorious woman! She should have been born English."

If she had been born English and led the English troops in France, the wars would have turned out differently; of that, Thomas Malory was sure. Instead . . . even now his mind would not let him recall the years after her death, the years of English losses, English defeats. It was as if the ashes and the heart of the Maid had become part of the river watering French soil that raised up a new generation of French men-at-arms against whom no English army could prevail. These new Frenchmen invented weapons that sent castles crumbling into ruins. English fighting spirit crumbled too. One by one, the great English leaders were killed in France or died there worn out by stress and disease.

The Duke of Bedford and the Earl of Warwick died at Rouen within a stone's throw of the square where the Maid had died. On April 30, 1439, in a high room of the castle, Richard Beauchamp died of the bloody flux as his liege lord King Henry V had died at the Bois de Vincennes. Over land and over water his body was carried, like the body of the great King, for burial in England.

Richard Beauchamp's bones lay in a stone coffer at the entrance of St. Mary's Church in Warwick until a chapel

Galahad

could be built to honor him. It took twenty years to build that chapel, and surely, thought Thomas Malory, there was no finer chapel in all of England and France. Its gleaming white walls and gilded arches protected the fair marble tomb on which lay an effigy of the great Earl, clad in armor of shining silver, his head bare and resting on a helmet. His hands were parted as if in adoration of some heavenly vision. His feet rested against a golden griffin and a golden bear. The bear and the ragged staff were carved in a decoration that circled the tomb, interspersed with words praising the Earl of Warwick.

But those words were pale compared with the ones which Thomas Malory now reread, looking over the final pages of his last story:

> Thou, Sir Launcelot, there thou liest, who were never matched by any earthly knight. And thou were the most courteous knight that ever bore shield! And thou were the truest friend to thy lover that ever bestrode a horse, and thou were the truest lover, among sinful men, that ever loved woman, and thou were the kindest man that ever struck with sword. And thou were the goodliest person that ever came among a throng of knights, and thou were the meekest and gentlest man that ever ate in hall among ladies, and thou were the sternest knight to thy mortal foe that ever put spear in rest.

With the death of Richard Beauchamp the long shadow of the Maid fell on the defenseless head of Henry VI, whom the Earl had trained and nurtured so carefully and led to his crowning as King of England and King of France. The King was now eighteen years old, a knight as pure and stainless as if Galahad had come to earth again. At that age his father had been a seasoned soldier. Men wondered what the son would make of his two kingdoms.

THE ENGLAND OF THOMAS MALORY
Bamborough
Alnwick
Leicester
Monks Kirby
Coventry
Warwick
Bury St. Edmunds
Northampton
Tewkesbury
Oxford
St. Albans
Barnet
London
Bristol
Bedwin
Amesbury
Dover
Glastonbury
Salisbury
Winchester
Hastings
Southampton
Wareham
Portsmouth
Tintagel
N

MORDRED

> "Lo, all ye Englishmen, see ye not what mischief was here? For he that was the best king and noblest knight of the world, and most loved the fellowship of noble knights, and by him they all were upheld, yet these Englishmen could not be content with him. Lo, thus was the custom of this land, and men say that we of this land have not yet lost that custom. Alas! this is a great fault of us Englishmen; nothing pleases us for long."
>
> THE MOST PITEOUS TALE OF THE MORTE ARTHUR
> SANS GUERDON

DURING his bachelor years in France, in the long lulls of many campaigns, Thomas Malory had been drawn to books, of which France could offer many more than England. He looked for old tales of King Arthur and found many, not only of Arthur, but of Merlin, of Launcelot, of Tristram, whom the French called Tristan, and of the search for the Holy Grail.

He also read several books on the proper behavior of women. A "Goodman of Paris," a householder, had written a fine one for his own wife. As he read, Thomas Malory had conjured up a picture of the perfect woman, and often dreamed about her. The goodman's wife was much younger than her husband, who wrote to her with tender memories of their first married days: "You being fifteen years old in the week when we were wed, begged me to excuse your youth and ignorance in your service to me until you had seen and learned more, which you promised to do diligently. You prayed me humbly, in our bed as I remember, that for the love of God I would not correct you harshly before strangers or before our servants, but that I would correct you each night and from day to day in our chamber and show you the unseemly things done in the day past and chastise you, if it pleased me, and then you would not fail to amend yourself according to my will, as you said. And I praised you and thanked you for what you said to me and I have often remembered it since."

It was a charming picture: the great bed with its curtains drawn; the little wife docile, confiding; the husband wise and indulgent. It pleased him for her to twine her garden roses and violets into wreaths for her hair, to dance, and to sing. But he had not forgotten that she wanted guidance; his book was written to teach all that a wife should do and be. He told her how to say her prayers and to make her confession to her priest, how to keep fleas out of the blankets, and how to order a supper for twelve in Lent, how to hire servants and manage them, how to get out grease spots, to clean furs, to examine horses for defects, and how to cook for an invalid. (The householder was sixty years of age.)

Wishing his wife to be happy and at ease in society, he gave her the rules for playing indoor games, and for hawking, the favorite outdoor sport of ladies. He added a list of

Mordred

riddles for her amusement. Coming to more serious matters, he warned her to shun the example of women who walked "with roving eyes and head reared up like a lion, their hair straggling out of their wimples." Head up, eyelids lowered, not fluttering, and looking neither to the right nor to the left, that was how she should walk in public places, doing honor to her husband by her fair, simple, decent array and her perfect manners. Such was the French model, mused Thomas Malory, wondering where he could find her like.

On his return to England in 1439 after the death of Richard Beauchamp, his family urged him to marry. He was near forty and his father was dead. The care of the Malory estates was now on his shoulders. Still he hesitated; for a soldier, a bachelor's life was best, he thought. In one of his stories Thomas Malory made Sir Launcelot say what he himself had felt in those days:

> To be a wedded man I think it not good, for then I must live with a wife, and leave arms and tournaments, battles and adventures. And as for taking my pleasure with lovers, that will I refuse in principle for dread of God . . . for he who takes lovers shall be unlucky, and all things about him shall be unlucky.

So he wrote, but the wars in France had been long and there had been plenty of French girls who welcomed English soldiers into their beds. He had taken his pleasure with them; he was punished now. He was unlucky, and all things about him were unlucky.

The difference between what he had meant to be and what he was! Even at the time it had troubled him, and now in the long silences of Newgate Prison it troubled him more. As a stream, long held back by sticks and stones, will burst through at last and rush along its course to the sea, so the old trouble burst from his mind and flowed from his pen in a story of Sir Launcelot.

"Sir," said the damsel, "a knight often comes along this road who distresses all ladies and gentlewomen. At the very least he robs them or lies by them."

"What?" said Sir Launcelot, "is he a thief and a knight? And a ravisher of women? He does shame to the Order of Knighthood, and contrary to his oath."

It was hard for a knight on campaign to keep that oath. Easier perhaps for Richard Beauchamp, who brought his wife and child to the castle of Rouen and made a kind of family life for himself there. Yet in the end each man was judged not by the difficulty but by the keeping of the oath.

Thomas Malory thought ruefully how slow he had been to marry. It was his family, not he, who had at last chosen Elizabeth for his wife. But he could not have done better. She was young, teachable, of gentle birth, and she owned a little property called Stormfield near Leicester. The Malorys living there knew and approved of her family, who were quiet folk, willing to send a suitable dowry with their daughter and to make no trouble.

He smiled now. When he first met Elizabeth, had she not looked rather like the young wife in Master Geoffrey Chaucer's tale?

> *Fair was this young wife, and withal*
> *As any weasel her body slim and small.*
> *She wore a girdle all of barred silk,*
> *An apron white as morning milk . . .*
> *She was more blissful for to see*
> *Than is the yellow pear tree*

> *And softer than the wool of any wether,*
> *And by her girdle hung a purse of leather . . .*
> *As sweet as honey or the mead her breath*
> *Or hoard of apples laid in hay or heath . . .*

Elizabeth had a high, clear voice and willingly sang with him when he came courting. She knew "The Nut-Brown Maid" from beginning to end, and taught him the part of the Earl's son who pretended to be a banished man in order to test his lady's love. Elizabeth with lowered eyelids demurely sang the lady's verses, always ending,

> *For in my mind of all mankind*
> *I love but you alone.*

The final verse they sang together in good spirit:

> *Here may ye see that women be*
> *In love meek, kind, and stable;*
> *Let never men reprove them then*
> *Or call them variable . . .*

From the first year of their marriage, when he had been gone from home as often as not, Elizabeth had managed everything. She made ends meet and found the money to pay the high taxes brought on by the wars. There were three estates besides her own Stormfield, each with its steward. Elizabeth watched the stewards, who watched the bailiffs, who watched the reeves, who watched the tenants, who watched the flocks and tended the fields. She saw to it that floors were strewn with fresh rushes and that garden walls were mended. She held courts at St. Edith's church and collected rents. She barred the doors and windows when roving bands of marauders came pounding on them, threatening to rob or rape her.

The countryside was full of such men, mostly soldiers returned from the French wars, homeless and idle. Many had never been paid for their services. Because he himself had later joined them and had done what he could for them, poor devils, he was in prison now. As boys, he and Philip Chetwynd had joyfully sung of how Robin Hood took from the rich to give to the poor, but the law never looked kindly on a Robin Hood. Through it all, Elizabeth had never wavered.

In fancy, he relished the thought of the fair cruel Lady Lyonet, who taunted poor Gareth for his great height, "like a weed standing higher than the good corn," but, in fact, how satisfying to see Elizabeth's eyes looking up with undisguised admiration as he towered above her. And the faraway princess, waving her hand from a high remote window, suited a tale of romance, but in real life he was grateful for the simple loyalty of Elizabeth, who wanted only to be close at his side. When he was away from home she wrote faithfully all that he needed to know. "To my right worshipful Husband Sir Thomas Malory, Knight, be this letter delivered in haste . . ." Her letters followed him wherever he went.

He was often at Warwick Castle in the service of young Henry Beauchamp, who had been loaded with honors and responsibilities by his king and close friend, Henry VI. Henry Beauchamp, now Thomas Malory's lord, was a most amiable young man, full of promise. Beauchamp had the good looks of his father and mother. As Thomas Malory remembered him riding out from the dark archway of the castle gate, he was like a burst of sunlight. From crested helmet to silver spur, he shone. Whenever he was known to be coming, the people of Warwick lined the road, waved their caps, and watched for his smile. They knew that his feeling for the Church had grown as he grew to manhood; they blessed him and tried to touch him, sensing holiness as he passed. Richard Beauchamp had been Warwick's Launcelot; his son was its Galahad.

Henry Beauchamp liked to make short pilgrimages by boat down the Avon from Warwick to where the river joined the broad Severn on its journey to the sea. A familiar pain stirred Thomas Malory's heart as he remembered that boat setting sail westward to the great abbey church of Tewkesbury, which the young Earl especially loved, saying that he wanted to be buried there. Long ago Sir John Malory's Welsh minstrel had sung of a quest by water toward the west in search of a mysterious life-giving Cup. All men prayed that someone young and peerless, like Henry Beauchamp, would find the Grail Cup, for if the Grail quest failed, so the stories told, only one thing remained, Armageddon, the last great battle before Judgment Day. How did "The Death Song" go? "The host of broad England sleeps with the light in their eyes . . ."

But the year 1440 was the time to think of life, not of death. Henry Beauchamp was soon to be married to the Lady Cecily Neville, daughter of the Earl of Salisbury. Richard Beauchamp's daughter Anne had already married a Neville and this second marriage would doubly unite the two powerful houses. Together they could carry everything before them, strengthening the loyalties of all who supported the young King Henry VI. Under his banner, after a hundred years of war, England would have peace.

First there was a matter of policy to settle. Both Beauchamps and Nevilles looked to two men close to the King who could make peace with France. One, Cardinal Beaufort, had crowned the King in Paris. The other was the Earl of Suffolk. Through their influence the Duke of Orléans was released from his long imprisonment and went home to France to urge the cause of peace. This move was strongly opposed by the Duke of Gloucester, who constantly urged his nephew the King to press forward with the war. Cardinal Beaufort and the Earl of Suffolk saw Gloucester as the greatest barrier to any hope of peace, and they saw how to remove him.

His marriage to Jacqueline of Hainaut had failed; he had long had a mistress, a beautiful woman named Eleanor Cobham, now his wife. It was said that she had made a wax figure of the King and held it to the fire, so that it melted away, bit by bit. If so, it was witchcraft, for the King's wits were becoming feebler day by day. He seemed unable to make decisions. Eleanor Cobham could be made to suffer for it. She was found guilty and was forced to walk through the streets of London for three days, barefoot and dressed in the long gray robe of a penitent. Gloucester's reputation was destroyed and he retired from public life, consoling himself by collecting books.

Humphrey, Duke of Gloucester, was a man who might have been King, a man of high culture, a brave soldier, wounded at Agincourt, pouring out his life's blood for his brother the great Henry V, and later, when fortune passed him by, devoting his energy to the best interests of his young nephew, as he saw those interests. Yet he was destroyed; only his books remained to honor him, and they were shut away from the noise and strife of the world in the quiet cloisters of Oxford, where Thomas Malory had seen them. He could think of the Duke with sympathy, for in his own disgrace he too had found much solace in books.

Mordred

Even with the Duke of Gloucester banished, there were still many who did not support the King. They were increasingly bitter over the losses in France. Year by year French towns were becoming French once more, as English armies withdrew in sullen defeat. At Pontoise in 1441 Charles VII, who called himself King of France, ordered three hundred English prisoners stripped, tied hand and foot, and flung into the Seine to drown. At home, year after year, English people poured gold into the King's treasury, and still his debts for the war were unpaid.

A French marriage for the English King might be a remedy for these woes. The Earl of Suffolk was sent to France to arrange a match. Before long came news that he had found a perfect wife for young Henry. She was barely in her teens but already she was beautiful, brilliant, charming. She would bring out the best in Henry or supply whatever might be lacking in him. Her name was Margaret of Anjou, so called for that part of France south of Brittany. Her father was making difficulties about the marriage settlement, but the Earl of Suffolk sent word that he was determined to win her for Henry's bride.

All in all, as the year 1444 began, Thomas Malory had good hope for the future. He was about to be sent to Parliament, representing Warwickshire. His wife, Elizabeth, was expecting a child. And Henry Beauchamp, Earl of Warwick like his father before him, would soon be created Duke. His wife had borne a little daughter; the Beauchamp line would go on, and there might yet be a son to carry on the name. As for the King, he was in better health and spirits, looking forward to his marriage.

The Christmas of 1444 was the last merry Christmas that Thomas Malory remembered at Newbold Revel. Robert, his son, was a newborn babe; Elizabeth, who had borne him with difficulty, her slender frame not being suited to easy birth, was tremulously joyful as she held their child. After Robert there had been no more children.

At Warwick the young Earl with his Countess celebrated the Twelve Days of Christmas in ancient splendor. They gave alms to the poor of Warwickshire who crowded at the gate all through the festive season.

With high hope as the new year opened, Thomas Malory had ridden off to London with his squire, young John Appelby, a good man, a loyal friend. At Coventry they were joined by Sir William Mountford, long in the service of Richard Beauchamp during the French wars. He was one of many who had married in France, bringing home a Breton lady to his estate at Coleshill.

South along the highroad to London the band of knights and squires made their way, stopping only where an abbey or an inn could give them a roof for the night, and bread and ale to stay their hunger. At last after a week's traveling they saw the towers of Westminster Abbey, in whose Chapter House the Commons would be meeting. Thomas Malory remembered ruefully that as they passed on to Newgate and paused at the guard room to give their names and state their business in London, a voice, cursing or praying, had shouted down from a cell of the prison.

Beyond Newgate the stink of the Shambles assailed the nose, and mongers of pepper and fish and cheese cried their odoriferous wares. But the wayfarers would not need to buy food. The gate of the vast Neville house stood open on the far side of the market and they were expected there as welcome guests. Richard Neville, the great lord who had

Mordred

married Richard Beauchamp's daughter, welcomed all comers of his acquaintance. He kept a household of six hundred men.

Thomas Malory was at once attracted to Richard Neville, whose tall figure, lean, well muscled, broad in shoulder, seemed made for action. He was still a youth, but his strongly aquiline features suggested nervous energy and ambition. He wore his black hair cut short like a soldier's and he had already proved himself a soldier. He was altogether a young man to Thomas Malory's taste; his manner, simple and open, was the same to all, no matter how they were dressed. (A poor knight from Warwickshire could not hope for a London coat sewn with seed pearls and worn over a shirt of white lawn fringed with gold like those he saw about him. A tunic of silk and a velvet cap would look well in Parliament, but they were not for Thomas Malory.)

He could not abide the new style of shoes with toes that turned up a full three inches. A man's stride would soon become a mincing step in such shoes. But he would have liked to make a better appearance. He could only hope that his long record of good service to Richard Beauchamp, in war and in peace, would count for more than fine clothes. Like Sir Balin at Arthur's court, he was still "poor and poorly arrayed. But in his heart he was sure he would do as well, if good fortune favored him, as any knight there."

At the end of February 1445 he had his first taste of Parliament and it was a bitter one. After debate that august body decreed that no man could hold a seat in Parliament unless he had an income of at least £40 a year. Thomas Malory's income was only half of that. But by the new law he might still serve if he was "a notable knight." His pride was sore as he made a list of those still living who remembered his services to Richard Beauchamp and might speak for him.

Fortunately, Philip Chetwynd, now a great man at the King's court, still lived and remembered. Philip, as it happened, had just been retained in the service of Humphrey, Duke of Buckingham. This was news indeed, for the Duke of Buckingham was also Earl of Stafford, that same Stafford who had wellnigh killed the Maid at Rouen as she lay in shackles before him. The Duke could be met, said Philip, if Thomas cared to look for him in the House of Lords. Thomas preferred to have a letter from Philip asserting that he was "a notable knight."

On the whole the year 1445 went well. Thomas Malory was proud to have been one of those who confirmed the King's grant for the building and endowment of a new school at Eton and a new college at Cambridge. And he was well satisfied that the money for the new schools would come from the dissolution of alien monasteries. There was hardly an Englishman who did not chafe at the thought of the gold that flowed yearly from England to France through those monasteries. Certainly, few had complained at home since the French ties of the monastery at Monks Kirby had been dissolved.

Thomas Malory was pleased too with the work of a royal commission on which he served arranging that the poorest towns of Warwickshire should be forgiven their taxes. As recently as Christmas he had seen the distress of hungry folk at Warwick Castle gate. Times were hard for everyone at home, but for these humble ones most of all.

On days when Parliament was meeting he walked or had himself rowed upstream from Paul's Stairs to the wharf at

Mordred

Westminster. Often when he stood on that wharf watching the busy traffic of boats on the river, he thought of the Fair Maid of Astolat. In the old French *Mort Artu* her body had been rowed down an unknown river to an unnamed city, but it might have happened here.

One of the last stories Thomas Malory had retold was that of the Fair Maid, and in memory of his year in London he called the river "Thames" and named the city "Westminster." He told how the lone oarsman "rowed the barge unto Westminster, and there it rubbed and rolled to and fro a great while ere any man spied it." Rubbed and rolled to and fro . . . a homely detail of the scene, but a true one. Rereading, he held his pen poised over the words, then let them stand.

In April, Margaret of Anjou reached Southampton with several hundred followers. There had been months of delay, since King Henry had offered to pay the whole cost of the bride's journey to England and was unhappily not able to find the money in his treasury. He had ended by pledging most of the crown jewels and much silver plate to pay the enormous sum.

News reached London that Margaret was gravely ill at Southampton. There was general consternation. She was well again. General rejoicing. There was a rumor that King Henry had gone to meet her disguised as a simple squire, kneeling before her with "a letter from the King." In this way he was able to take in every feature of her vivacious face while she never looked at him. She kept him kneeling all the while she read the letter. There was a similar story of how King Arthur had first wooed Queen Guinevere disguised as a gardener's boy. Many said that Arthur and Guinevere had come again.

The wedding took place with all speed at Tichfield Abbey near Southampton. As May came on with its fresh flowers, the royal pair moved joyfully toward London along roads crowded with loyal folk pressing to touch the hems of jeweled robes. The fields were white and gold with the daisies called "marguerites" and the people paved Margaret's path with them.

She rode to St. Paul's Cathedral in a chariot drawn by two white horses with trappings of white damask powdered with gold. Her dress too was white and gold and her hair, crowned with gold and pearls, hung shining to her shoulders.

On the last day of May, Margaret of Anjou, dazzling all beholders, was crowned Queen of England at Westminster Abbey. By her side moved the King, his mild face radiant. Grateful for his happiness and good fortune, he created earldoms and dukedoms for the friends closest to him. Henry Beauchamp became Duke of Warwick.

But the King's bliss was short-lived. By the end of the year the court knew the price which the Earl of Suffolk had paid for the bride. He had ceded to France the great province of Maine, which lay between Anjou and Normandy and which had long been safely held by English soldiers. Thomas Malory remembered the sense of stunned disbelief, then of outrage, as the news traveled from mouth to mouth.

For soldiers like himself, the loss of Maine was unforgivable, but in his personal life another grief overshadowed all else. In 1446 Henry Beauchamp died. He was twenty-two years old. In the French book, Galahad beheld

Mordred

the Holy Grail, received the Body of Our Lord in communion from the hands of Joseph of Arimathea, and was carried straight to heaven by flights of angels. So it seemed the young Duke had gone also. So brief a life, so full of promise. Thomas Malory left London and returned to Warwick for the funeral of his lord.

According to the Duke's wish, the boat carrying his body moved westward, downstream, for the last time to the abbey church at Tewkesbury. As he had seen it then, Thomas Malory saw it again in his mind, rereading what he had written of Galahad's last prayer:

> Lord, I thank Thee, for now I see what hath been my desire many a day. Now, my Blessed Lord, I would live in this wretched world no longer, if it may please Thee, Lord.

Henry Beauchamp had done well to leave this wretched world in all the perfection of his youth. Better to die young, thought Thomas Malory, than to grow old as his friend Henry VI of Lancaster, the high prince, was to grow old, in gathering shadows. For through his marriage came the loss of Maine, and with the loss of Maine a long darkness fell over England. This shadow overwhelmed the King.

The pay for members of Parliament was small. Expenses were high. Thomas Malory came home to Newbold Revel poorer than when he had left for London, and he had no lord to follow. But his cousin Philip Chetwynd died during the same year, and Thomas Malory found himself drawn into the service of the Duke of Buckingham, with whom Philip Chetwynd had stood high. Thomas Malory was not much pleased to be counted as one of Buckingham's men,

KNIGHT PRISONER

but the Duke offered him a seat in Parliament representing a borough in Wiltshire, and beggars could not be choosers.

So it happened that he was called to Bury St. Edmunds north of London in February of 1447. Parliament was being summoned there for a special meeting to confront the Duke of Gloucester, who was thundering angry protests against the loss of Maine. He was, after all, heir to the throne unless the King had a child, and he was lashing out at Suffolk, whose management of affairs in France seemed to him no less than treason.

It was a ride of seventy-five miles in winter weather from Newbold Revel southeast to Bury St. Edmunds, but Thomas Malory thought nothing of that. He was only taken aback to find a large force of the King's men-at-arms camped to the north of the town and to learn that they were there by the Queen's orders. Both the King and the Queen were at that moment present in the town. Thomas Malory's own orders directed him to the inn where the Duke of Buckingham would lodge. There to his astonishment he heard that Gloucester was to be arrested on arrival.

Parliament was meeting in the abbey of Bury St. Edmunds and there the issue was soon made clear. On the night of February 18 Thomas Malory heard that the Duke and a band of his friends had been taken as prisoners to the tower of the abbey. The Queen brought grave charges against Gloucester. She accused him of usurping the rights of the King and charged that he was plotting with Richard, Duke of York, to seize the throne for the house of York.

Four days later the Duke of Gloucester was found dead in his prison. The shock of his death was profound. There were no marks on the body or other signs of violence, but rumors of murder persisted. It was clear that the Queen could hardly conceal her satisfaction. Now her favorite, Suffolk, could move toward the ratification of his pledge to give Maine back to France and so conclude a peace at last. Thomas Malory returned to Monks Kirby deeply disturbed. The King was in the hands of fools, while his Queen, a French woman after all, served France.

Helpless to stem the tide of affairs, Thomas Malory found consolation the following year at Warwick, where a new chapel at St. Mary's Church was rising stone by stone, most beautifully, in memory of Richard Beauchamp. In a room of the church tower a man named John Rous was gathering a library to honor the Beauchamp family, and Rous became a friend. He was writing a history of the Earls of Warwick and showed Thomas Malory some curious genealogies which he had brought back from a pilgrimage to Glastonbury Abbey. The monks there said that Joseph of Arimathea, bearing the Holy Grail, had traveled the long weary way from the Holy Land to Glastonbury and at journey's end had thrust his staff into the ground. He had married a daughter of the very Roman soldier who had pierced Our Lord's side. More wonderful yet, the records showed that Igraine, the mother of King Arthur, was descended from Joseph of Arimathea. And, most wonderful of all, King Arthur and Queen Guinevere had been buried in Glastonbury's ancient abbey. There was a legend that Arthur would return, and the monks, in order to quiet the ever restless and rebellious Welsh, had opened the grave to prove that Arthur was dead. No one knew where his bones now rested, but the story lived. Pilgrims crowded the road to Glastonbury, hoping to glimpse the Holy Grail or at least to see the place of the graves and the thorn tree that blossomed each year at Christmastime where Joseph of Arimathea had planted his staff.

John Rous had a copy of Geoffrey of Monmouth's history, in which could be read the stories of Merlin and of Arthur's wars. He had the writings of Wace, who had put Geoffrey's *Chronicle* into verse and had spoken of the Round Table. He had a volume of Layamon, who had embroidered on Wace's work. One after another John Rous brought out his books for Thomas Malory, who read avidly. His personal affairs sorely needed attention, but he snatched every possible moment to steep himself in John Rous's books.

The Duke of Buckingham owned vast properties in Wiltshire and Dorset, King Arthur's country. When in 1449 the Duke named him as representative to Parliament for a Wiltshire borough called Bedwin, Thomas Malory had a sense of quest, even though the quest would force him to leave home at a bad time. Henry Beauchamp's little daughter, Anne, had died, and the title and Beauchamp estates were passing into the hands of Richard Neville, who would now be Earl of Warwick through his marriage to Richard Beauchamp's daughter. Richard Neville was no friend to the King. With ties to the Duke of Buckingham and to the new Earl of Warwick, Thomas Malory's loyalties were divided. It was not to his liking. One good lord, one clear cause to follow, was all he had ever asked. Now all was a tangled web. It was a painful memory still and had found its way into his tale of Merlin:

> Then stood the realm in great jeopardy a long while, for every lord that was mighty of men made himself strong and many thought to become king.

Mordred

Once again, unable to stop the turn of Fortune's wheel, he had turned away, leaving the burden of family responsibilities on Elizabeth's shoulders. He kissed her and small Robert, who clung to his mother's skirts. His friend and lieutenant John Appelby would do what he could for their safety. Thomas Malory rode off south to Bedwin.

It was high summer. In upland fields cattle browsed quietly and Wiltshire farmers, peaceful as their cattle, were haying or mending fences and hedges. Little did they know or care about wars and rumors of wars among earls and dukes so long as they could harvest their crops and eat their hard-earned bread unmolested. But at Bedwin Thomas Malory heard complaints. Soldiers home from France were riding through Wiltshire, robbing and plundering. Could not the King protect his people? And what was Parliament for if not to maintain law and order?

Thomas Malory did not know the answers to these troubling questions. He soon rode on to Winchester for another look at the Round Table, which still hung in the great hall of the castle. Had Winchester been Camelot? Yes, he could dimly see lettering around the table's edge—Arthur, Launcelot, Gareth, Galahad, Mordred—In his own lifetime he seemed to have known all of them, all but Mordred.

England would soon have its Mordred. But as yet, in that unclouded summer of 1449, Mordred was only a name for evil in the old tale of how Arthur had fought his last battle near Salisbury. Thomas Malory turned his horse's head to the west and to that ancient city. At the end of a day's easy riding he looked down on the roofs that clustered around the spire of the great cathedral, on the river Avon circling the town, and on its water meadows. Impossible to tell now where Arthur's last battle had been fought. The tales told how two knights had carried the king "to a little chapel not far from the sea." Time changes all things; in a thousand years even the course of the river, the coast itself, might have changed.

Thomas Malory rode slowly through the town, crossed the bridge that spanned the river, and stood long, looking into the silvery stream. As in a mirror he saw the slender spire of the cathedral reflected there. Was this the water side from which Sir Bedivere threw the king's sword Excalibur? Was it from here that the little boat had carried the king to Avalon? Some of the old stories said that Excalibur had disappeared into a lake; some, into the sea. "Some men say . . ." That was as near as he could get to the truth of the matter. The monks at Salisbury were collecting a great library and there Thomas Malory found books about King Arthur and his knights and about the adventure of the Holy Grail. He never forgot the books he had seen at Salisbury on that pilgrimage of twenty years ago.

If the visit to Salisbury was unforgettable, it was followed by others even more so, for he had gone on to the edge of Salisbury Plain, where stood Stonehenge, high, windswept, and as solitary as Merlin, whose magic had built it. How else could those giant stones have risen, if not by magic?

Almost within sight of Stonehenge lay Amesbury, where, if the legends were true, Queen Guinevere, grieving for the death of the king, had become a nun, and lived out her life in prayer and penance. If it was true . . . if, if! The nuns at Amesbury Abbey told him that the queen had indeed sought refuge here. They offered to show him a wimple which she had worn and to let him read their books

Mordred

concerning the Holy Grail. It was all convincing, and it led him irresistibly on to Glastonbury. He had known all along that he must go to Glastonbury.

Now, in Newgate Prison, Thomas Malory added a note. In his last pages telling of Guinevere's death and of Launcelot's sad pilgrimage to carry her body on its final journey, he wrote that it was a ride of little more than thirty miles from Amesbury to Glastonbury. Those who might read his work would see that he knew whereof he spoke.

Westward from Amesbury the air grew softer and fragrant with the scent of apple trees. The Romans had called Glastonbury "Insula Avalonia," the Isle of Apples, for it had once been almost an island, surrounded by river and marshland. The ground had been given to the earliest monks by King Arthur himself. Thinking of these things, Thomas Malory fell into a sweet and dreamlike trance as he rode toward the shrine of his pilgrimage. He was not disappointed. The monks of Glastonbury were most explicit in answer to his questions. They told him that on Easter Monday of the year 1278 King Edward I and his Queen Eleanor had witnessed the remains of King Arthur, which the monks of that time had exposed at the request of the royal pair. The bodies of Arthur and Guinevere had then been placed in wooden caskets and buried behind the high altar. So the records showed in the great library of the abbey, and so the monks still said. And yet, Thomas Malory thought, as he rode back to London, Glastonbury was not the final answer. Legend said that there was another Avalon where Arthur was not dead but was healed of his wounds and would come again.

He had read all the books and asked all the questions. Now he could only say:

> Thus of Arthur I find never more written in books that be authorized, nor more of the certainty of his death I never heard tell . . . Yet some men yet say in many parts of England that king Arthur is not dead, but had by the will of our Lord Jesu in another place. And men say that he shall come again, and he shall win the holy cross. I will not say it shall be so, but rather I will say, here in this world he changed his life . . . But many men say that there is written upon his tomb this verse, HIC IACET ARTHURUS REX QUONDAM REXQUE FUTURUS.

Here lies Arthur the once and future king. The reader must decide for himself.

The dream world of Glastonbury had turned into a nightmare when Thomas Malory once again faced the real world of London. Meetings of Parliament were tumultuous as news came in October that Charles VII of France had led an army to Rouen and that a mob inside the walls had seized the gates and handed the city over to him. In December Harfleur fell under an attack from the new and powerful French artillery.

In a bitter mood Thomas Malory rode home to Newbold Revel, where Elizabeth told of disaster piled on disaster. John Appelby had nearly been murdered by a gang who roamed the roads or lay in ambush in woods and barns. They were a mixed lot, men of title and commoners. They called themselves a "fellowship" as if they were Robin Hood's merry men, but there was nothing merry about them. What with their thefts and the cruelly high taxes, the farmers could not pay their rent and the bailiffs were deep in disputes. Not long since, a troop of men, led by a knight in armor, had ridden into the courtyard of Newbold Revel, stolen horses, and pulled down the stable before they rode away. It would be a sorry Christmas.

John Appelby laid much blame for the plight of the farmers at the doors of Coombe Abbey and Monks Priory, where the monks were suspected of felony and even of rape. Whether true or not, these suspicions added to the resentment over goods and gold that were heaped up in monastery coffers. Even the Holy Church admitted that the monks were a disgrace. A bishop chided: "The divine office, by night and likewise by day, is neglected; obedience is violated; the alms are wasted; hospitality is not kept. There is nothing else here but drunkenness and surfeit, drowsiness—we do not say incontinence—but sloth and every other thing which is on the downward path to evil and drags men to hell."

At the beginning of January 1450, John Appelby rode to Newbold Revel with more than twenty men mounted and armed. They said that they had grievances and intended to set wrongs right. Thomas Malory's age, strength, and military experience made him their natural leader, if he would join them. They intended to begin by attacking Coombe Abbey and raiding its treasury. He hesitated, saying that an act against the abbey was a crime against the King, who was head of the Church. Not so, they told him. With the King surrounded by villains and powerless against them, it was every man for himself and the devil take the hindmost.

Sir Baldwin Mountford was one of the company. His grievance was severe; it exposed corruption in high places. His father's Breton wife had bribed the Duke of Buckingham in a plot to steal the family property at Coleshill for her own son, displacing Sir Baldwin, the true heir. This perfidy settled it for Thomas Malory. He agreed to lead the new fellowship.

On the night of January 4, the riders gathered in the woods near Coombe Abbey. At a signal they moved silently toward the abbey gates. Suddenly there was a clatter of hooves on the road from Coventry and in the glare of torches another band of riders appeared. Even in the uncertain light Thomas Malory recognized Humphrey Stafford, Duke of Buckingham. The Duke spurred his horse and passed through the gate to safety while some of his followers bolted it behind him. The others, swords and daggers drawn, were left in a melee with Thomas Malory's friends, but the skirmish ended without bloodshed. That was the first night of many such nights.

Thomas Malory had thought that he was not recognized, for that autumn the Duke of Buckingham named him as Member of Parliament representing the little town of Wareham in Dorset. Meanwhile, numerous grievances had been righted in and around Monks Kirby. That summer the fellowship had broken into houses four times and forced the restoration of goods and money they deemed their own.

How easy it was to go on, once they had begun, how easy to justify every raid! They went scot-free, perhaps because the armed forces of the law were occupied with greater malefactors. Suffolk's enemies were demanding his head to pay for the loss of Maine. He had grown rich and corrupt; Parliament wanted him imprisoned at the very least. But Queen Margaret planned for him to get to the safety of exile in France. Off the coast of Kent a pirate ship seized him; his captors cut off his head and mounted it on a pole.

Mordred

With Suffolk's death a reign of terror began. In Kent a soldier of fortune named Jack Cade gathered an army of farmers, fishermen, merchants, and knights. They called themselves loyal subjects of the King, but they marched to London, demanding the blood of the King's evil advisers. "His merchandise is lost," they said, "his common people is destroyed, the sea is lost, France is lost, the king oweth more than any King of England owed."

The King's army was ambushed by the rebels, and Henry and Margaret fled to the north. Jack Cade's men were howling for reform, but at the same time they committed atrocities. They dragged the Bishop of Salisbury from his altar, murdered him, and stripped him to the skin. In London they slew high officials and carried their heads through the city. They looted and burned. No city in France had received worse treatment. The fires burned out at last and Jack Cade's army dispersed. There was talk of pardon for all of them, but Cade himself was slain before he reached home.

Parliament would reconvene in London during November. Thomas Malory again rode south, this time to Dorset, to see the town he represented. He was uneasily aware that the common people were grumbling about such appointments as his; they demanded to elect their own representatives as they had done in times past. However, they did not trouble him long, for he was soon gone from Wareham on a quest that meant more to him. Wareham was an ancient town lying in a harbor on the south coast. He took passage in a ship sailing for Cornwall. His horse was hauled to a stall deep in the waist of the vessel.

At night the sun set in the western sea. Every cloud on that horizon might be the island called Avalon, the golden

Apple Isle, where Arthur still lived. The sailors knew of no such island, but they told him that they would sail near the islands sometimes called Lyonesse, off Land's End. There had once been more land there, now lost beneath the sea except for mountaintops. The air was so balmy that strange trees and fruits grew there, seldom seen in northern lands. Perhaps his island of Avalon was somewhere in Lyonesse. Or perhaps it had sunk entirely beneath the waves. No one could tell.

Thomas Malory had not yet come to the end of his pilgrimage. King Arthur's birthplace lay ahead. Two days after they turned northward along the coast of Cornwall, he saw Tintagel. It was a day of high wind and waves that dashed raging against steep cliffs, veiling them with clouds of foam. He stared into the mist. Was it an abbey or a castle that he saw? He could not be sure; it was in ruins now. At least he had seen it.

After Tintagel he fell into talk with a sailor from Somerset who had the fey look of a Celt. Ah, said the fellow, if you wanted to know about King Arthur, you should see a place near his home. There was a hill and a spring, and on Midsummer Eve you could hear the hoofbeats of King Arthur's horse going to be watered at the spring as it had gone before the last battle. It was shod with silver shoes. No, said another sailor, that battle was in Cornwall, and Arthur was buried not far from Tintagel. He knew the lake into which Bedivere threw the sword. That was near Tintagel. All of the sailors knew about Arthur. They all knew different places where he had fought or where he was buried.

The ship docked at Bristol, where Thomas Malory took to the road again and made for London. He was not des-

Mordred

tined to stay there through all the meetings of that Parliament. In March he learned that a warrant was out for his arrest. Last summer's crimes had come home to roost. Thinking that he might as well be hung for a sheep as for a lamb, he went home to help his fellowship settle old accounts. During June and July they took several hundred head of cattle and sheep. They also drove some deer from a park belonging to the Duke of Buckingham.

Here Thomas Malory's luck ran out. He and John Appelby were captured and turned over to a sheriff, none other than Sir William Mountford, who locked them up at Coleshill. It had been easy to climb through the window that night and dive into the moat below. The next day they had been home in time to join a dozen men in settling the account at Coombe Abbey. They took all they could carry and returned the day after with a hundred men to take more.

On August 23, 1451, an inquisition was held at Nuneaton a few miles north of Coventry. The Duke of Buckingham presided and listened to charges made formally against Thomas Malory. At the same time the sheriffs of London sent officers to Newbold Revel with a writ ordering him to appear before the King at Westminster to answer these charges. He read them with anger. "Malefactor and breaker of the king's peace . . . extortion . . . felony . . ." He was not guilty. He had taken the law into his own hands only because there was no justice in the land. Then, incredulously, he read the last two charges: "That Thomas Malory, knight, on the Saturday before Pentecost, 1450, broke into the house of Hugh Smyth at Monks Kirby and feloniously raped Joan, the wife of the said Hugh. That Thomas Malory, knight, on Thursday, August 1, 1450, feloniously raped Joan, the wife of Hugh Smyth, at Coventry, and carried away goods and chattels of the said Hugh, to the value of £40."

Rape was the unforgivable crime, one for which a soldier of Henry V would have been hanged without delay. Even now a charge of rape would so damage his reputation that no good light could be put on the other charges. If anyone of his fellowship was guilty of rape, it was not Thomas Malory. "What," said Sir Launcelot, "is he a thief and a knight *and* a ravisher of women?" But the charge was enough. There was no way to disprove it.

Still, he would answer the charges. He declared to the King's officers that he was not in any wise guilty and that he would stand trial. From that time on, the law had played a cat-and-mouse game with him. In London's Marshalsea Prison, out on bail. Imprisoned at Colchester in Essex and out by a violent break, armed with dagger and sword. Sent to Ludgate, to the Tower. Pardoned, and back to the Marshalsea for lack of bail. In Newgate and out again. Wherever he went, they found him, and no one rose to protect him. He was too strong to be pitied. Through it all, he never blamed the King. He loved his King and forgave him, seeing him as a saint and a victim of the events that followed in the next terrible years.

By 1452, Richard, Duke of York, was maneuvering to seize the throne, but, strong as he was, even he did not dare to test the love of the people for their anointed King. The Queen had now given birth to an heir to the throne, a beautiful boy named Edward, but the following year the King's mind gave way under the stress of his sorrows and the old shadow of his Valois heritage. The Duke of York became Lord Protector of the little prince. The house of York

Mordred

was gaining strength every day, for many expected the King to die and remembered what misery it meant to have a baby as king.

Then in 1454, as suddenly as he had lost his reason, the King regained it. His friends rallied to his cause, wearing a red rose to show allegiance to the house of Lancaster. Yorkists answered by wearing a white rose. Richard Neville, Earl of Warwick, wore the white rose, but, like many others, professed to be the enemy not of the King but of his advisers.

Open war between the two houses broke out with a battle at St. Albans in 1455. It was a Yorkist victory, but still Henry VI remained King, and the Queen bided her time. Year after year there were battles and uneasy peace between battles, while anarchy spread terror throughout the kingdom. Like two knights parrying and feinting, the houses of Lancaster and York tried their strength against each other, each waiting for an opening to make a final, fatal thrust.

The King wanted peace. He prayed for peace; he did penance and fasted. In 1460, captured by Yorkist forces at Northampton, he was taken ceremoniously to the Tower of London, where, in the cause of peace, he granted the crown to the Duke of York after his own lifetime. Charles VI had done the same for Henry V in France, disinheriting the Dauphin. Now Henry VI disinherited his son Edward, Prince of Wales. But he acted without the Queen's consent. Like a tigress she defended the birthright of the heir, leading an army of Lancastrians to fight the Yorkists at Wakefield in the north. There, Lancaster had always been strong. After a resounding victory the Queen ordered, "No quarter." There was a massacre as the house of Lancaster avenged itself. The war cry was "By God's blood, thy father slew mine; and so will I do thee, and all thy kin." Many Yorkist lords were killed without mercy. The Duke of York died with one of his sons.

But he had another son, named Edward, and now a new generation of Yorkists rose up around this boy. The Queen remained in the north. The new Duke of York entered London. His father had pretended loyalty to Henry VI, but Edward proclaimed himself king. He was young and handsome, dressed in a gown trimmed with ermine. Around his neck was a collar of jewels set in gold. His golden hair was perfumed and hung to his shoulders, yet the people could see that he was not effeminate. They knew him to be a hot-blooded soldier, gallant and daring, and his claim to the throne was as legitimate as that of Henry VI. They hailed him as King Edward IV. To Thomas Malory, he was Mordred.

With the crowning of Edward IV came a general pardon, and Thomas Malory found himself free. He went home to Newbold Revel and was soon called by Richard Neville, Earl of Warwick, to join a military expedition being gathered to attack fortresses in Northumberland at Alnwick and Bamborough.

Thomas Malory answered the call. Richard Neville had risen as a power greater than either Edward or Henry. He was linked by birth and by marriage to both Lancaster and York. He had behind him the wealth of the Beauchamp estates and the high name of Warwick. For his support and his valor in battle Edward IV was granting him great favors and Richard Neville was conducting negotiations for a marriage between Edward and the sister-in-law of the new

Mordred

king of France, Louis XI. The bear and ragged staff once again meant supreme power.

Thomas Malory had had doubts about the proposed French marriage. The English had a weakness for French women, it seemed, and he could remember none who had not brought trouble. Even Joan of Arc, whom they had burned to ashes, was rising to haunt them. The triumphant French were holding a new trial with the intention of finding her innocent of every charge brought against her. But French wife or no, the great question remained: Was Edward IV "rightwise born King of England?"

In the Tower of London Henry VI said sadly to his Yorkist guardians, "I have been King. My father was King; his father was King. You have all sworn fealty to me on many occasions, as your father swore it to my father." But he could never be king in any real sense. He was only the figure around whom Lancastrian hopes gathered. It was Queen Margaret alone who pressed on with single-minded savagery and led Lancastrian forces to battle after battle, while Henry, once again freed, was taken like a statue, venerated and protected, to places of safety nearby. In 1460 the Duke of Buckingham died protecting Henry VI.

Henry VI was to sink still lower. Lancastrian hopes faded, and the Queen and the young Prince barely escaped with their lives, penniless, to France. Henry was captured again and was led as a laughingstock through London, wearing an old straw hat, his feet tied together under his horse. Thomas Malory had seen Joan of Arc enter Rouen shackled in the same way, but riding with more dignity. Henry Beauchamp had died young like Galahad, the son of Launcelot. If his friend and king, Henry VI, had ever resembled that other Galahad, "the high prince" of the old tales, the resemblance was long since gone. Henry VI was not fortunate enough to die young.

One by one, in successive Yorkist or Lancastrian defeats, the flower of England's nobility was dying, by battle, murder, and sudden death. Often their bodies were beheaded and left to lie, stripped naked, where they fell. Still the war went on. In defeat, the leaders of both sides retreated to France to ask help from Burgundy, or from Louis XI. Queen Margaret, risking everything to secure England's throne for her son, asked help from Scotland, England's immemorial enemy. She even mortgaged Calais, England's last French stronghold with its rich revenues, in exchange for aid from Louis. Against the obsessive rage of this woman Richard Neville pitted his strength.

Thomas Malory had loyally followed him north to Alnwick and Bamborough on the Scottish border in the bitter cold of December 1462, eight years before. He had fought through three months of snow and biting wind, of scant food and sleepless nights. But that was nothing compared with the death of his son, Robert, who, briefly married and a father, had died in the fighting. Bamborough was said to have been Launcelot's castle of Joyous Gard. In the last pages of his final story he would add a line or two telling how Launcelot when he was dying "prayed the bishop that his fellows might bear his body to Joyous Gard. (Some men say it was Alnwick, and some men say it was Bamborough.)" He hoped that Richard Neville would remember what the Malory family had done there.

Richard Neville's support of Edward IV had soon been paid with double-dealing. While he was still working to unite the King with a French wife, Edward secretly married an English lady, Elizabeth Woodville, whose father had been no more than a steward of the Duke of Bedford. And while Warwick was trying to arrange an alliance with French diplomats, Edward secretly concluded one with Burgundy. The King had made a fool of Warwick both at home and abroad. Furthermore, Elizabeth Woodville had a large family, and Edward gave them titles. With the titles went political power. The King had already surrounded himself with merchants and other commoners who appeared more and more often in the luxurious court where the young King was drinking heavily, eating enormously, and having his way with every woman who struck his fancy. The old order was changing, and Edward IV found that Richard Neville was no longer for him, but against him.

Neville prepared for a stand to the last ditch. All over England his followers rose, and were ruthlessly suppressed. Like many others, Thomas Malory found himself again in prison, but the Earl was still free. In this very year of 1469 he had done what no one thought could happen. He had gone to France to reconcile himself with Queen Margaret and to propose that Prince Edward, her son, should marry his daughter Anne. Margaret, now living on the charity of the French King, could not at first believe this proposal of her bitterest enemy, but the old hope rose in her and she at last consented, much encouraged by promises from the French King.

On a piece of the True Cross in the cathedral of Angers, chief city of her own Anjou, the Earl of Warwick swore to serve King Henry, the Queen, and the Prince as long as life lasted. The King of France swore to aid Warwick in the cause of King Henry. And Queen Margaret vowed that she would never reproach the Earl for his past offenses against her. When King Henry was restored to his throne, the marriage would take place between the Earl's daughter and the Prince of Wales.

Bit by bit this news came to Thomas Malory as he finished his work in the ninth year of the reign of King Edward IV. In February 1470, King Edward again issued a royal pardon to many persons, as he had done on numerous occasions in the past, but again, as before, he excluded Thomas Malory, by name, from his pardon. There would never be any pardon for him from Edward now. Warwickshire was still a Lancastrian stronghold and Thomas Malory had too many friends to be safely set free there; even in his old age he could be a rallying point for the Earl of Warwick.

In September Richard Neville landed with an army on the southwest coast of England and marched to London under banners emblazoned with the bear and ragged staff. King Edward was in the north, where another Lancastrian uprising had taken place. As he turned and marched south to meet the invaders, he was taken by surprise. A turncoat army threatened to seize him and send him as captive to the Earl of Warwick. With nothing but the clothes they wore, Edward and a few followers sailed for Burgundy. That same day Richard Neville entered London and ordered Henry VI released from captivity.

At the end of November Parliament met for the first time since 1467. Lancastrian rights and properties were restored, and Thomas Malory received his pardon. He had no word from the Earl of Warwick himself, but he believed that the Earl, or someone acting for him, had read the last

Mordred

tale in his collection and remembered Alnwick and Bamborough.

He had not the strength to go home, but if the Greyfriars would have him, he could go to them. He would have to be carried, but the Greyfriars would do it. If he had been younger and stronger, he would have asked them to take him as a lay brother, but they would take him out of mercy as an invalid. How many times he had written of good monks and hermits who ministered to knights sick or wounded in battle!

They would give him a cell not very different from a prison cell. He would eat coarse food not very different from prison food. But the brothers would care for him tenderly. Perhaps when they could find the time to do it, they might carry him in to see the great library from which his books had come.

He would like to tell John Rous about the library at Greyfriars Abbey. Rous was now a priest at Guy's Cliff. Thomas Malory would not see Guy's Cliff again, or Warwick Castle, or Newbold Revel. But he might see Elizabeth again. If she came to London he would tell her to bury him in the chapel of St. Francis at Greyfriars Abbey. No need to take his body home. And for an inscription, nothing but his name, the date of his death, a mention of Monks Kirby, and perhaps a word or two about his service. It might not be too much to say "brave soldier"; the monks would put it in Latin, "valens miles." He would be remembered for nothing else, if he was remembered at all.

The Lancastrian Claim to the Throne

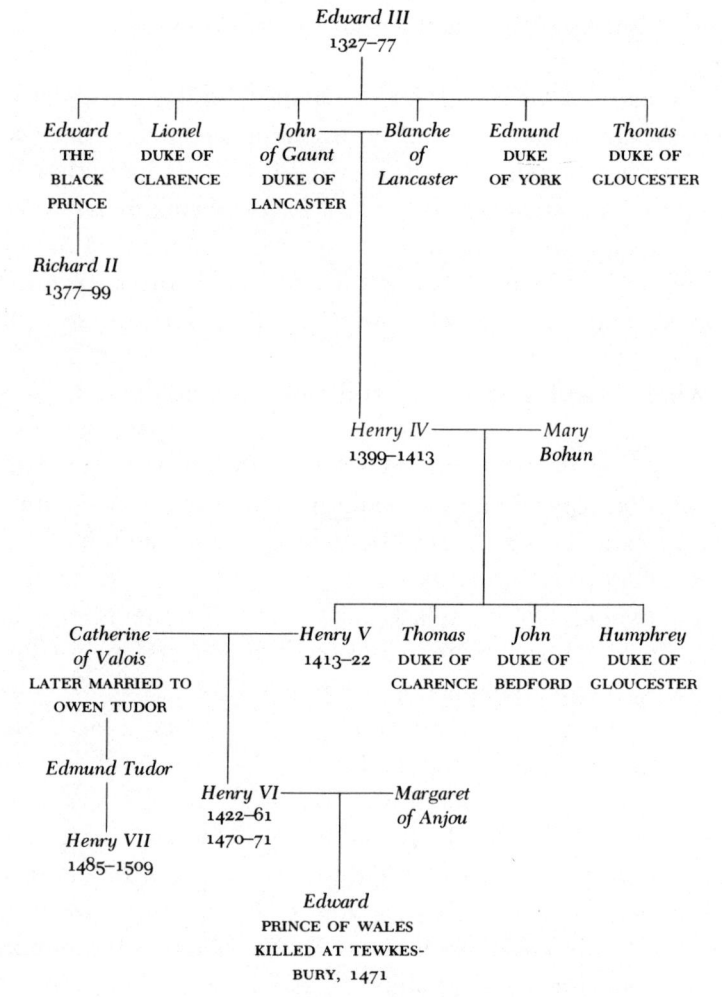

Edward III
1327–77

- **Edward** THE BLACK PRINCE
  - *Richard II* 1377–99
- **Lionel** DUKE OF CLARENCE
- **John of Gaunt** DUKE OF LANCASTER — **Blanche of Lancaster**
  - *Henry IV* 1399–1413 — *Mary Bohun*
    - *Catherine of Valois* LATER MARRIED TO OWEN TUDOR — *Henry V* 1413–22
      - *Edmund Tudor*
        - *Henry VII* 1485–1509
      - *Henry VI* 1422–61, 1470–71 — *Margaret of Anjou*
        - *Edward* PRINCE OF WALES KILLED AT TEWKESBURY, 1471
    - *Thomas* DUKE OF CLARENCE
    - *John* DUKE OF BEDFORD
    - *Humphrey* DUKE OF GLOUCESTER
- **Edmund** DUKE OF YORK
- **Thomas** DUKE OF GLOUCESTER

The Yorkist Claim to the Throne

Edward III
1327–77

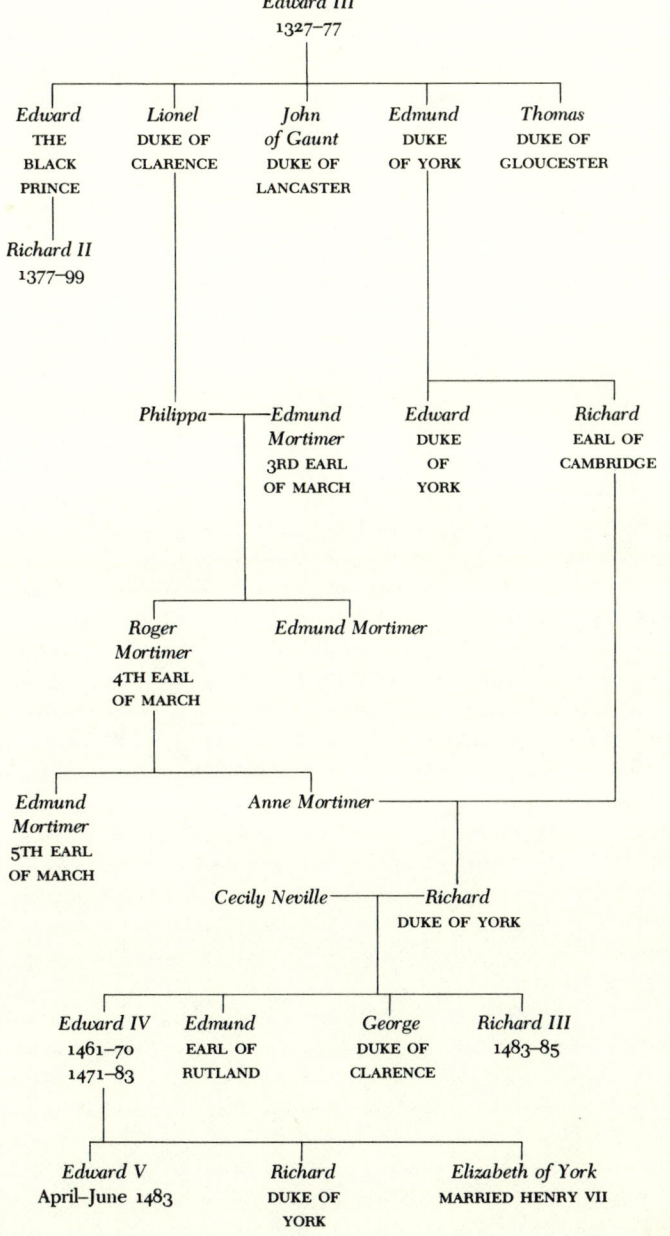

- **Edward** THE BLACK PRINCE
  - **Richard II** 1377–99
- **Lionel** DUKE OF CLARENCE
  - Philippa — **Edmund Mortimer** 3RD EARL OF MARCH
    - **Roger Mortimer** 4TH EARL OF MARCH
      - **Edmund Mortimer** 5TH EARL OF MARCH
      - Anne Mortimer
    - Edmund Mortimer
- **John** of Gaunt DUKE OF LANCASTER
- **Edmund** DUKE OF YORK
  - **Edward** DUKE OF YORK
  - **Richard** EARL OF CAMBRIDGE
- **Thomas** DUKE OF GLOUCESTER

Anne Mortimer married Richard (son of Richard, Earl of Cambridge)

Cecily Neville — **Richard** DUKE OF YORK

- **Edward IV** 1461–70, 1471–83
- **Edmund** EARL OF RUTLAND
- **George** DUKE OF CLARENCE
- **Richard III** 1483–85

Children of Edward IV:
- **Edward V** April–June 1483
- **Richard** DUKE OF YORK
- **Elizabeth of York** MARRIED HENRY VII

MALORY

"Of all the creatures on this earth, only man has asked Questions; only man endlessly pursues the Dark Bird of Unknowing, gathering up each feather his shafts loosen from the great wings. Feather by feather, he seeks to conquer his prey, and in so doing, to unravel the riddles governing his own world, and the worlds beyond, if such there be."

FRANCES CLARKE SAYERS, "MYTHS AND LEGENDS," IN
ANTHOLOGY OF CHILDREN'S LITERATURE

THE gravestone, worded in Latin, read: In the chapel of St. Francis under the fourth stone below the second window lies Sir Thomas Malory, a brave soldier who died on the fourteenth of March in 1470, A.D.* from the parish of Monks Kirby in the county of Warwickshire.

Soon after Malory's death, Richard Neville was killed in a Yorkist victory at Barnet near London. In another Yorkist victory at Tewkesbury, the young Prince of Wales was cap-

---

* 1471 according to the Gregorian calendar.

Thoreau's words, a part of history "is mythology always." Beneath the facts of a man's life and times we sense something more, the mythical forces that spell out destiny, for good or ill, as our modern eyes see it.

As one reads the *Morte Darthur*, the sense of meaning and destiny is inescapable, and the reader is free to make whatever connections he sees between the book and the life of the author. I cannot say with certainty, "Here Malory was thinking thus and so; at this point he was remembering a particular scene in his own life." But like all writers, Malory had to create from what he had consciously experienced as well as from his subconscious intuitions. Valid connections between Malory's life and his writing must exist, and they provide one of the few ways in which flesh can be put on his bones.

Another possible way is to compare him with Sir John Paston, a central figure in the famous Paston letters, which give us one of the best pictures of life in fifteenth-century England. Like Malory, John Paston was sometimes in prison during the Wars of the Roses; he too was "an absentee husband." Albert H. R. Ball, an editor of the Paston letters, has noted that family life in the fifteenth century was lacking in sentiment, but that Paston was evidently well liked; his wife wrote how much sympathy was stirred up at home by his imprisonment. He never gave up his fight against "the malicious ingenuity of his enemies." The Pastons, like the Malory family, wanted a steady government; they too supported the Lancastrian cause. Like Thomas Malory, John Paston had to ask for a pardon from Edward IV. Albert Ball sums him up as "an adventurous soldier, a careless business man, a patron of literature." Thomas Malory seems to have been much like John Paston.

Where facts are lacking in the tangle of the fifteenth-century wilds, my guides have been tradition and imagination, which can be astonishingly useful. Long after Troy had been given up as myth and only myth, the city itself was found where tradition and imagination had said it should be. Camelot may one day be found in the same way, and the old tales may help us to find what remains of its once-splendid towers.

Now and again in documents the name of Thomas Malory appears, but in a variety of spellings, perhaps referring to different men. Then for years at a stretch no such name can be found even by the most diligent search. The man simply drops out of sight. Malory's plight is like that of Shakespeare; hot arguments persist as to his identity. How could Shakespeare, an itinerant player, a man with "little Latin and less Greek," have written plays that reveal one of the most profound minds the world has ever known? And how could a criminal in his cell, a man accused of robbery, rape, and attempted murder, have written the *Morte Darthur* which we attribute to Sir Thomas Malory? The end of these controversies is not in sight, but it seems that prison, if you can buy or beg a few necessaries from the jailer, is an excellent place in which to write.

Like its author, the *Morte Darthur* has been the subject of much controversy. Professor Eugène Vinaver, foremost of Malory scholars, has shown that Malory intended to write eight separate "books" rather than a single volume. Yet C. S. Lewis, Professor Vinaver's friend and admirer, has pointed out that it is "as a mirror of honour, as a feast of marvels . . . as a romance of chivalry haunted by the higher mystery of the Grail, and as (in some sort) a unity, that the *Morte Darthur* has pleased. And not only pleased, but so far outstripped its rivals that it alone of all medieval prose romances has survived as a living book into our own century."

Whether it is one or eight separate books, the immortal charm of the *Morte Darthur* lies in the figures of Arthur and his knights. Their fascination seems irresistible to a very wide modern audience. Arthur, Merlin, Galahad, the names still echo from the May Day freshness of the enchanted forest. Through its branches the elusive figures still shine as if we could break through and find them alive, Gareth and Gawain, Guinevere and the Lady of the Lake, in a golden world close at hand. And Mordred, name of dread, still casts his long shadow across the brightness, foretelling the end.

The Arthur of historical fact remains a riddle; indeed, for some years the scholars said, "There was no Arthur, at least no proof of any Arthur." But scholarly opinion has changed. We believe in Arthur not as the Middle Ages saw him and as Malory wrote of him, the ideal king, clad in shining armor with all the trappings of chivalry, but as Winston Churchill saw him when he wrote in *The Birth of Britain*:

> Modern research has not accepted the annihilation of Arthur. Timidly but resolutely the latest and best-informed writers unite to proclaim his reality. They cannot tell when in this dark period [during the last days of Roman Britain] he lived, or where he held sway and fought his battles. They are ready to believe however that there was a great British warrior, who kept the light of civilization burning against all the storms that beat, and that behind his sword there sheltered a faithful following of which the memory did not fail . . . If we could see exactly what happened we should find ourselves in the presence of a theme as well founded, as inspired, and as inalien-

able from the inheritance of mankind as the *Odyssey* or the Old Testament. It is all true, or it ought to be; and more and better besides.

When the theme is inspired, history easily passes over into mythology and our interest grows. The unsolved mysteries of Malory's life may tease our curiosity and the power of his book command our attention, but the greatest lure is the mythical Arthur and the idea of kingship. This was felt long before Malory's time. By the twelfth century Arthur was already a British hero, "the once and future king," the national Messiah who would come again and save his people. Whichever king sat on the real throne of England, Arthur on his mythical throne was far more famous. It was written of him in those days: "What place is there within the bounds of the empire of Christendom to which the winged praise of Arthur the Briton has not extended? The eastern peoples speak of him as do the western, though separated by the breadth of the whole earth." Our own nation's capital became "Camelot" not so long ago.

Malory, a fifteenth-century man, working on "the French book" in his prison cell, would not have troubled himself much about what was Arthurian fact and what was fiction, as we do today. C. S. Lewis has said in *The Discarded Image* that belief or disbelief was seldom uppermost in the minds of medieval writers. What mattered was to hand on the stories of the past. "As the spaces above us were filled with daemons, angels, influences, and intelligences, so the centuries behind us were filled with shining and ordered figures, with the deeds of Hector and Roland, with the splendours of Charlemagne, Arthur,

Priam, and Solomon . . . Things were once better than they are now."

This glorious past was seen by medieval writers in terms of medieval life. Malory knew that Arthur had not worn fifteenth-century armor, but he *saw* him that way, and so felt closer to him. As C. S. Lewis put it, "Historically as well as cosmically, medieval man stood at the foot of a stairway; looking up, he felt delight. The backward, like the upward glance exhilarated him with a majestic spectacle, and humility was rewarded with the pleasure of admiration . . . The saints looked down on one's spiritual life, the kings, sages, and warriors on one's secular life, the great lovers of old on one's own amours, to foster, encourage, and instruct."

Although modern readers may see Malory more as the victim of a corrupt society than as a villain, he himself probably took full blame for his actions. With King Arthur and his knights looking down on Malory's secular life, he must have bitterly repented his sins in the words of the Bible: "For the good that I would I do not; but the evil which I would not, that I do." In the long ugly struggle between the houses of Lancaster and York, while many men were losing not only their lives and their fortunes but also their sacred honor, the ideal of perfect kingship and perfect knighthood must have been even more significant and compelling than ever.

Surely Malory had seen the Round Table at Winchester. He believed that he had known an ideal king in Henry V and an ideal knight in Richard Beauchamp. But the figure of Arthur meant more than an ideal king. Unconsciously he was identified with the divine powers of the primitive Celtic god, Artaius. And behind Artaius shone the glory that

C. S. Lewis called the "elusive Form which if once seen must inevitably be desired with all but sensuous desire—the thing (in Sappho's phrase) 'more gold than gold.' " Malory desired that thing. It is the repentant sinner who is most moved by the idea of perfection.

In Malory's day the Hundred Years' War and the divisive Wars of the Roses gave focus to the sense of sin and the vision of perfection. In our time, hell has disappeared and the sense of sin has been almost trained out of us by psychology and psychiatry. But alas for us, when hell went, heaven seems to have gone too, while the yearning for it remains. The great modern psychologist Carl Jung acknowledged this when he wrote: "All ages before ours believed in gods in some form or other. Heaven has become empty space to us, a fair memory of things that once were. But our heart glows, and secret unrest gnaws at the roots of our being."

This is why we respond to the legends of Arthur. This is why we cannot rest until we can answer the question "Who was Sir Thomas Malory?"

Afterword

> *"I have after the simple conning that God hath sent to me, under the favor and correction of all noble lords and gentlemen, enprised to imprint a book of the noble histories of the said King Arthur . . . and of certain of his knights, after a copy unto me delivered, which copy Sir Thomas Malory did take out of certain books of French, and reduced it into English."*
>
> FROM WILLIAM CAXTON'S PREFACE TO THE
> MORTE DARTHUR, 1485

WILLIAM CAXTON said in his preface that "many noble and divers gentlemen" had demanded that he should print the story of the Grail and the history of Arthur because he had already published books about other "great conquerors and princes." He did not tell who had delivered Malory's manuscript to him. Perhaps they were supporters of Henry VII, who became king in 1485. Caxton told of a conversation which he had with the noble gentlemen, when he suggested that Arthur might not have been a real person. The gentlemen, "and one in special," said that this was folly and blindness. They spoke of Arthur's grave at Glastonbury, of Arthur's seal in the shrine of St. Edward at Westminster, of the Round Table at Winchester, and of many references in ancient books. Evidently Caxton was convinced by these arguments.

On one memorable day of my long quest following the elusive figure of Sir Thomas Malory through the tangle of fifteenth-century history, I came to the Pierpont Morgan Library in New York. The vault was opened by special arrangement for my benefit, and a librarian brought from it the only complete copy of the *Morte Darthur*, that "noble and joyous book" which Caxton edited and finally printed fourteen long years after Malory's death.

The copy in the Morgan Library had been bound in red leather, decorated with gold, for the library of Sir Robert Harley, who bought it from its previous owner for two shillings and sixpence. It would be vulgar to guess what the price of this priceless book might be today.

I carefully turned the pages from first to last. Here was the story of Arthur's birth at Tintagel. I had climbed with my husband up and down the rugged cliffs above Merlin's cave in the rocky inlet that guards the approach to the legendary site of the castle. Surely, at some point in his life, Malory would have tried to see Tintagel.

I read the familiar story of how Arthur pulled the sword from the stone and was chosen king. Malory says that Arthur did this most famous of all his deeds "in the greatest church of London (whether it were Paul's or not, the French book maketh no mention)." Neither St. Paul's nor Westminster look now as they did then, but when we read about London in the *Morte Darthur* we can be certain that

Afterword

Malory was writing about places which he himself knew well.

Here was the tale of Sir Gareth and his devotion to Sir Launcelot, so much like the feeling of Malory for Richard Beauchamp, Earl of Warwick, if tradition and imagination were guiding me rightly. We had visited the grounds of Newbold Revel, once Malory's home, and taken pictures of St. Edith's Church, still standing at Monks Kirby. Coombe Abbey still stands too, on the road to Coventry. We counted the miles from there to Warwick Castle, where the librarian, Mr. P. A. L. Pepys, was generous with his time and help. We wandered through the high-ceilinged rooms and the gardens with their formal flowerbeds and strutting peacocks. We saw the dungeon and the torture chamber. Here Richard Beauchamp had lived from time to time, between wars and affairs of state. Arthur and Launcelot; Henry V and Beauchamp. When I read of Launcelot, I saw Beauchamp.

The wars in France! Wherever Richard Beauchamp fought, we had followed as well as we could, for where he was, there Malory may have been too. Professor Vinaver has shown how Malory changed the route of Arthur, as given in the old English *Morte Arthure* to match (closely enough) the route taken by Henry V in his French campaign. At Harfleur we found a breach on the seaward side of the ancient walls. We could be standing at the spot where Shakespeare's Henry V shouted to his knights: "Once more unto the breach, dear friends, once more; / Or close the wall up with our English dead!" Now I was reading the Fifth Book of the *Morte Darthur,* in which King Arthur determined to conquer the lands of the high and mighty Roman Emperor, saying, "I pretend to have and occupy the sovereignty of the empire wherein I am entitled by the right of my predecessors." So Henry V had said to Charles VI of France. I read how King Arthur took a city with "rearing of ladders, breaking of walls, and the ditch filled," and I knew that this was fifteenth-century warfare such as Malory himself saw during his military service with the Earl of Warwick in France.

No one has given me the slightest encouragement to imagine that Malory was at Agincourt—except Shakespeare, and he has given the tantalizing picture of the Boy, who talked to the soldiers before the battle and who was about the age that Malory would have been in 1415, a youth in his teens. I read in the *Morte Darthur* how the Lady Elaine said: "My lord, Sir Launcelot, at this same feast of Pentecost shall your son and mine, Galahad, be made knight, for he is fully now fifteen winters old." Was there a personal reference here, a clue to Malory's age on his first military expedition? Was he, after all, at Agincourt, perhaps with the baggage, like Shakespeare's Boy? I imagined how it might have happened.

It seemed not impossible. The historian Sir William Dugdale says that Malory served "at the siege of Caleys in King Henry V's time, being of the retinue of Richard Beauchamp." This reference has given some trouble, since there was no siege of Calais in Henry V's time. But a siege was expected in 1414 and this is the clue that I have followed. Richard Beauchamp was at Harfleur and went from there to England, taking the sick, the wounded, and prisoners. He must have taken some of his men with him on this operation, but others of his retinue might have returned to Calais, which was their regular post of duty. If so, they

Afterword

would have joined the march north with the King, who was heading toward Calais when he met and defeated the French at Agincourt. In this circumstance, Malory may have been with him. I have taken the liberty to believe so.

When our quest led us to France, we found Agincourt, although the French do not point tourists the way to the site of that humiliating defeat. We found Maisoncelles, where the English baggage was kept behind the lines during the battle. Was Thomas Malory with the squires and pages who guarded the baggage until the French overran them? King Henry was outraged when he heard that young boys had been killed at Maisoncelles. I have had to imagine what Malory saw, if he was there. If he was not there, he certainly was among the first to read what had happened. The King's chaplain kept the record and he was an eyewitness of the battle. He was stationed behind the lines with the baggage at Maisoncelles.

Three times in the *Morte Darthur* there are scenes in which a woman is to be burned at the stake, but each time the victim is saved at the last moment by a brave and gallant knight. Richard Beauchamp, that "Father of Courtesy," was in command at Rouen when Joan of Arc was burned at the stake. Malory is thought to have been there too. My husband and I stood in the square at Rouen where Joan was martyred. We entered the tower where she was shown the instruments of torture. We cannot know what Malory saw in his mind as he wrote repeatedly about women undergoing trial by fire; we do know what everyone at Rouen saw on May 30, 1431.

Newgate no longer stands. Greyfriars Abbey is gone with its great library from which Malory presumably borrowed the "French book" and others as sources for his work. Malory's grave in Greyfriars chapel is gone. But the Round Table still hangs on the wall of Winchester Castle's great hall, and the supposed site of Arthur's grave remains. We have walked over the quiet lawn beneath the broken arches of the abbey at Glastonbury. "Here lies Arthur the once and future king."

At the Morgan Library I turned to the end of the Caxton *Morte Darthur* and found Malory's Explicit, the final words added by an author to summarize his book or to ask for the good wishes of his readers. In the ancient spelling I made out the meaning:

> Here is the end of the whole book of King Arthur, and of his noble knights of the Round Table, that when they were whole together there was ever an hundred and forty. And here is the end of the Death of Arthur. I pray you all gentlemen and gentlewomen that read this book of Arthur and his knights from the beginning to the ending, pray for me while I am alive that God send me good deliverance, and when I am dead, I pray you all pray for my soul; for this book was ended the ninth year of the reign of king Edward the Fourth by Sir Thomas Malory, knight, as Jesu help him for his great might, as he is the servant of Jesu both day and night.

Then Caxton had added his own note:

> Thus endeth this noble and joyous book entitled le morte Darthur/ Notwithstanding it treateth of the birth/ life/ and acts of the said king Arthur/ of his noble knights of the round table/ their marvelous quests and adventures/ the achieving of the holy grail/ & in the end the dolorous death & departing out of this world of them all/ which book was reduced into English by Sir Thomas Malory knight as afore is said/ and by me divided

Afterword

into xxi books chaptered and printed/ and finished in the abbey Westminster the last day of July the year of our Lord M/CCCC/lxxx/V.

The book itself spoke the final words: Caxton me fieri fecit. (Caxton caused me to be made.)

In the isolation of his prison cell, Thomas Malory probably never saw a printed book, but when he died the printing press was about to come to England. As early as 1456 Gutenberg had printed a Bible at Mainz. Six years later, printed books were seen in Paris. In 1476 William Caxton returned to England from Bruges and the following year was printing books from his press in Westminster.

Other manuscripts by Malory may yet be found, perhaps the original one in his own writing. But even if this happens we shall not have solved all the problems. What of the "French book" that lay on the table beside him, and the other books that he used as sources? They too must have been based on still older manuscripts, and no written text was half as old as the tales themselves, woven in and out by generation after generation of storytellers, carried from England to France, to Germany and Italy, then back to England, richly embroidered at each stage of the journey, more intricately beautiful for all their travels.

To most of us the *Morte Darthur* is simply Malory's gift, "deeply loved, darkly understood." It is only for scholars to try to trace the labyrinthine ways of its sources. We know that Malory did not add much that was new to the old stories remembered from childhood or retold from the "French book." He did not need to. There are, after all, very few story themes. Those which we have are told over and over, with variations. Only the scenery, the costumes, and the actors change as the centuries pass; the themes were the same in Malory's day as in ours. Courage, constancy, hopes betrayed, the changes of Fortune's wheel, love, death, he had known all of them. And he had followed the Dark Bird of Unknowing through the enchanted Arthurian forest. He found some of its feathers. And when he held them in his hands, he spoke with the voice, vital and passionate, that still moves us, the voice from the great deeps, of the "knight prisoner."

Acknowledgments

I have many people to thank for help they have given in the writing of this book and many gave help without my knowing their names. My deep appreciation goes to librarians at the Carnegie Library of Pittsburgh, in the Hillman Library and the Elizabeth Nesbitt Room at the University of Pittsburgh, at the Pierpont Morgan Library and the Thomas J. Watson Library of the Metropolitan Museum of Art in New York. In England I was allowed to consult the awesome resources of the British Library in the British Museum, and in France the Cabinet des Manuscrits of the Bibliothèque Nationale and the archives of the Bibliothèque Municipale in Rouen.

More especially I thank Mr. P. A. L. Pepys, Librarian at Warwick Castle, Miss Monica Ory in the County Records Office at Warwick, Sister Mary Peter, St. Paul's College of Education, Newbold Revel, Warwickshire, and M. Lucien Saint, Directeur Administratif of the Mairie de Calais, France.

I have been overwhelmed with the generosity of scholars whose work is related to Sir Thomas Malory or to the fifteenth century. First and foremost of these has been Professor Eugène Vinaver, whose correspondence with me came at a time when he was under great pressure of work and travel. His cordial and encouraging letters were far beyond my deserving.

At Professor Vinaver's suggestion Professor P. J. C. Field of the University College of North Wales at Bangor wrote to me in a full and friendly way answering questions which showed his awareness of the problems I faced in sorting out speculation from fact.

Mrs. Dorothy Styles in Warwick is writing a book about Richard Beauchamp and took time from her own research to help me with mine.

Sir Robin Mackworth-Young of the Royal Library at Windsor guided me to Maurice Bond, Honourable Custodian of the Muniments at St. George's Chapel, whose work has covered a piece of information that greatly interested me although it did not find its way into this book. According to the records of St. George's Chapel, the heart of St. George, which the Emperor Sigismund gave to Henry V, was kept in the Chapel with other relics of St. George, including a piece of his head. By an extraordinary bit of luck I knew where the rest of his head was. In May 1971 Dr. Kenneth M. Setton, the husband of my Vassar College roommate, had discovered in the abbey on the island of S. Giorgio off the mainland from Venice "the top of a skull, with a gold band encircling it . . . There was an inscription on the band [which] identified the relic as the cranium of St. George." Dr. Setton works at the Institute for Advanced Studies in Princeton. In an address to the Mediaeval Academy of America in April 1972 he described the excitement of the discovery, which his wife shared. My years on the trail of Sir Thomas Malory have been full of such delights as this.

Acknowledgments

At Carnegie-Mellon University Dr. Ludwig F. Schaefer and Dr. Carl I. Hammer of the Department of History and Philosophy have very kindly read the chapter which concerns the Wars of the Roses. Dr. J. Phillip Immroth of the Graduate School of Library and Information Sciences at the University of Pittsburgh filled in essential details about the earliest days of printing in France and England.

In 1974 I made a pilgrimage to Columbus, Indiana, to meet Dr. Stith Thompson, who talked to me about his career as a folklorist. During this visit I mentioned Malory, and Dr. Thompson told me that he himself was descended from the Beauchamp family. He gave me an invaluable genealogy which had appeared in the Filson Club History Quarterly for April 1954. He knew about the dedication of this book before the illness which ended with his death in January 1976.

As always, my last and best thanks go to my husband, Fletcher Hodges, Jr., who through all my wanderings has indulged my every whim, shared my pleasure in every discovery, and loaned me his powers of logic and memory from beginning to end.

Pittsburgh, Pennsylvania
January 1976

Bibliography

Altick, Richard D. "The Quest of the Knight-Prisoner," in *The Scholar Adventurers*. New York: Macmillan, 1950.
Anderson, John L., comp. *A Fifteenth Century Cookry Boke*. New York: Scribner, 1962.
Ashe, Geoffrey. *King Arthur's Avalon, the Story of Glastonbury*. London: Collins [1957].
────── *King Arthur in Fact and Legend*. Camden, N.J.: Nelson [1971].
Bagley, J. J. *Margaret of Anjou*. London: H. Jenkins, 1948.
Baker, Timothy. *Medieval London*. New York: Praeger, 1970.
Baugh, A. C. "Documenting Sir Thomas Malory," in *Speculum*, VIII (1933).
Bédier, Joseph. *The Romance of Tristan and Iseult*, trans. Hilaire Belloc and Paul Rosenfeld. New York: Heritage, 1960.
Bennett, Jack Arthur Walter, ed. *Essays on Malory by Walter Oakeshott et al*. Oxford: Clarendon, 1963.
Buchan, Alice. *Joan of Arc and the Recovery of France*. New York: Macmillan, 1948.
Bulwer-Lytton, Edward. *The Last of the Barons*. New York: Scribner, 1903.
Chambers, Sir Edmund Kerchever. *Arthur of Britain*. New York: Barnes and Noble [1964].
* Chrestian de Troyes. *Arthurian Romances*, trans. W. Wistar Comfort. London: Dent, 1913.

* Primary source

Churchill, Winston S. *The Birth of Britain*, History of the English-Speaking Peoples. New York: Dodd, 1956.

Clemens, Samuel Langhorne. *Personal Recollections of Joan of Arc, by the Sieur, Louis de Conte* [pseud.] *(her page and secretary)*. New York: Harper, 1926.

Dickens, Charles. *A Child's History of England*. London: Chapman & Hall, n.d.

Doyle, Sir Arthur Conan. *The White Company*. New York: McKay, 1958.

* Dugdale, Sir William. *Antiquities of Warwickshire, Illustrated*. London: Thomas Warren, 1656.

Field, P. J. C. "Sir Thomas Malory, M.P.," in *Bulletin of the Institute of Historical Research*, Vol. XLVII, no. 115. London: Univ. of London, 1974.

Fletcher, Robert Huntington. *Arthurian Material in the Chronicles, Especially of Great Britain and France*. New York: B. Franklin [1958].

* Froissart, Jean. *Froissart's Chronicles*, ed. and trans. John Jolliffe. London: Harvill, 1967.

* Geoffrey of Monmouth. *History of the Kings of England*, trans. Lewis Thorpe. Baltimore: Penguin, 1966.

Hamilton, Franklin. *Challenge for a Throne, the Wars of the Roses*. New York: Dial, 1967.

Harnett, Cynthia. *The Load of Unicorn*. London: Methuen, 1959.

* *Henrici Quinti, Regis Angliae, Gesta*, ed. Benjamin Williams. Vaduz: English Historical Society, 1964.

Hibbert, Christopher. *Agincourt*. Philadelphia: Dufour, 1964.

Hicks, Edward. *Sir Thomas Malory, His Turbulent Career*. Cambridge: Harvard, 1928.

* *High History of the Holy Grail*, trans. Sebastian Evans. New York: Everyman's Library, n.d.

* *History of the Press-Yard*. London: T. Moor, 1717.

* Huscher, H. *John Page's Siege of Rouen*. Leipzig: Kölner Anglistische Arbeiten I, 1927.

Hutchison, Harold F. *King Henry V*. New York: Day, 1967.

* Primary source

Bibliography

Jacob, E. F. *Henry V and the Invasion of France.* New York: Macmillan, 1950.

Kent, William. *Encyclopaedia of London,* rev. ed. London: Dent, 1951.

Kittredge, George Lyman. "Who Was Sir Thomas Malory?" in Harvard Studies and Notes in Philology and Literature, v. V (1897).

Lewis, C. S. *The Discarded Image: An Introduction to Medieval and Renaissance Literature.* Cambridge: Cambridge, 1964.

Loomis, Roger Sherman, ed. *Arthurian Literature in the Middle Ages.* Oxford: Clarendon, 1959.

Lumiansky, Robert Mayer. *Malory's Originality.* Baltimore: Johns Hopkins [1964].

The following editions of Malory are of special interest:

* Malory, Sir Thomas. *King Arthur and His Knights, Selections from the Works of Sir Thomas Malory,* ed. by Eugène Vinaver. Boston: Houghton [1956].

* *King Arthur of Britain* from Sir Thomas Malory's *Morte Darthur,* arranged by Brian Kennedy Cooke. Illuminated in the style of early English miniatures by Anthony Rado. Leicester: Ward [1954].

* *Le Morte Darthur.* Westminster: Caxton, 1485.

* *Le Morte Darthur,* ed. by H. Oskar Sommer with an essay on Malory's prose style by Andrew Lang. London: Nutt, 1889-91. (Caxton's text reprinted page for page, line for line.)

* *Le Morte Darthur,* modernized as to spelling and punctuation by A. W. Pollard. New York: Heritage [1955].

* *The Works of Sir Thomas Malory* in 3 v., ed. by Eugène Vinaver. 2nd ed. Oxford: Clarendon, 1967.

Maynadier, Gustavus Howard. *The Arthur of the English Poets.* Boston: Houghton, 1907.

* *Le Ménagier de Paris,* trans. Eileen Power as *The Goodman of Paris.* London: Routledge, 1928.

* *Merlin, or the Early History of King Arthur,* 2 v. London: Early English Text Society, 1899.

* Primary source

* Nicolas, Sir Nicholas Harris. *History of the Battle of Agincourt.* New York: Barnes and Noble, 1970.
* *Pageant of the Birth, Life and Death of Richard Beauchamp, Earl of Warwick,* ed. Dillon and Henry St. John Hope. London: Longmans, 1914.
* *Parisian Journal 1405–1449,* trans. from the anonymous *Journal d'un Bourgeois de Paris* by Janet Shirley. Oxford: Clarendon, 1968.
* *Selections from the Paston Letters,* trans. Sir John Fenn, and ed. Albert H. R. Ball. London: Harrap, 1949.
* Pernoud, Régine. *The Retrial of Joan of Arc: The Evidence at the Trial for Her Rehabilitation 1450–1456,* trans. J. M. Cohen. New York: Harcourt, 1955.

Power, Eileen Edna. *Medieval People.* Harmondsworth: Penguin, 1937.

Pyle, Howard, *Men of Iron.* New York: Harper, [c 1919].

Reiss, Edmund. *Sir Thomas Malory.* New York: Twayne [c 1966].

Robertson, D. W. Jr. *Chaucer's London.* Princeton: Princeton U., 1968.

* *Romances of Sir Guy of Warwick and Rembrun His Son,* ed. from the Auchinleck Ms. Edinburgh: Printed for private circulation, 1840.
* Rous, John. *A Pictorial History of the Earls of Warwick,* ed. W. Courthope. London: 1845 [–59].

Scherer, Margaret R. *About the Round Table.* New York: Metropolitan Museum of Art, 1945.

* Scott, W. S. *The Trial of Joan of Arc, Being the Verbatim Report of the Proceedings from the Orléans Manuscript,* trans. with an intro. and notes. Westport: Associated Booksellers, 1956.

Shaw, George Bernard. *Saint Joan.* Seattle: U. of Washington, 1968.

* *Sir Lancelot of the Lake: A French Prose Romance of the Thirteenth Century,* trans. Lucy Allen Paton. London: Routledge, 1929.

Snell, F. J. *King Arthur's Country.* London: Dent, 1926.

Stanislaus, S. M. *Newbold Revel, A Warwickshire Manor.* Leicester: St. Paul's College, n.d.

Stevenson, Robert Louis. *The Black Arrow, A Tale of the Two Roses.* New York: Scribner, 1955.

* Primary source

Bibliography

* Stow, John. *Survey of London,* ed Ernest Rhys. London: Dent, 1912.
* Strassburg, Gottfried von. *Story of Tristan and Iseut,* trans Jessie N. Weston. London: Nutt, 1907.
* Trask, Willard. *Joan of Arc, Self Portrait.* New York: Stackpole, 1936.

Victoria History of the Counties of England. London: U. of London Institute of Historical Research, n.d.

Vinaver, Eugène. *Malory.* Oxford: Clarendon, 1929.

* Wace. *Arthurian Chronicles by Wace and Layamon,* ed. Ernest Rhys. New York: Dutton, 1928.

Warwick, Frances Evelyn, Countess of. *Warwick Castle and Its Earls, from Saxon Times to the Present Day,* 2 v. London: Hutchinson, 1903.

* Primary source

Index

Agincourt, 39, 56, 61–7, 70–1, 73–4, 165, 176–7
Alnwick, 154, 156, 159
Amesbury, 144–5
Angers, cathedral of, 157
Anjou, 7–10, 88, 133, 157, 164
Appelby, John, 134, 143, 146–7, 151
Aquitaine, 57
Arcturus, 3
Armageddon, 131
Armagnac, Count of, 109
Armagnacs, 42, 73, 75, 79
Arthgal, 20
Arthur, xii–xiii, 3, 5, 9, 15, 16, 20, 25, 30–5, 40, 44, 46, 55–6, 65, 93–4, 96, 125, 142–145, 168–71, 175–6; death of, 66–7, 94–6, 144; sword of, 67, 144, 150, 174; grave of, 95, 141, 145–6, 174, 178; and Guinevere, 97–8, 120–1, 137–8, 141, 145; birthplace of, 150, 174; *see also Morte Darthur*
Astolat, Fair Maid of, 137, 176
Avalon, 144–5, 149–50
Avon River, 131, 143

Balin, 135
Ball, Albert H. R., 166
Ball, John, 12–13, 106
Bamborough, 154, 156, 159
Barflete, 55
Barnet, 163
Battle Abbey, 10
Baugé, 88

Beauchamp, Anne, 133, 142
Beauchamp, Elizabeth, 87, 101
Beauchamp, Henry, 102, 119, 130, 131, 133–4, 138–9, 142, 155
Beauchamp, John, 43–4, 46, 51, 57, 61, 64, 72, 81
Beauchamp, Richard, Earl of Worcester, 101–2
Beauchamp, Richard, 3, 6, 14, 40, 135–6, 141; and Malory, xii, 19, 21–2, 26, 30, 47–8, 76, 78, 103, 107–8, 131, 135, 136, 165, 170, 175–7; fame and nobility of, 8, 19–20, 26, 75, 76; and pages, 21–2; wife of, 21–2, 24–5, 39, 87, 101, 128; and war, 25–6, 29, 42, 76–9, 81, 84, 88–90, 118–19, 175–6; and Calais, 26, 28–9, 42, 46, 72, 176–7; and Henry V, 26, 40, 75–6, 84, 91, 120; and Joan of Arc, 31, 34, 109–12, 114–16, 119–20; children of, 38, 87, 101–2, 118–19, 128, 131, 142, *see also under names of*; and tournament, 46–8; returns to England, 56, 85, 176; and Henry VI, 102, 104, 107, 120; death of, 122–3; *see also* Warwick Castle
Beauchamp, Thomas, 27–8
Beaufort, Cardinal, 119, 131–2
Beaumains, 48
Bedford, Duchess of, 111
Bedford, Duke of, 91, 103, 105, 106, 109, 119, 122
Bedivere, 66–7, 94, 144, 150
Bedwin, 142–3
Birth of Britain, The, 168–9

INDEX

Black Prince, 28–9
Blangy, 60
Bois de Vincennes, 89–90, 92, 98, 122
Bosworth Field, 164
Bourbon, Duke of, 59, 71, 74–5
Bristol, 150
"Brother of the Quill," 70
Buckingham, Duke of, 136, 147, 148, 155; Malory and, 139–40, 142, 148, 151
Bunyan, John, xi
Burgundy, Duke of, 42, 58, 73, 75, 78, 80, 83, 89, 91, 103, 106, 108
Bury St. Edmunds, 140

Cade, Jack, 149
Caen, 76–8
Calais, 26, 28–9, 39, 42–3, 46, 72, 75, 93, 107, 156, 176–7; as key to France, 26, 45; burghers of, 27, 54; English army and, 45, 51, 54, 56–9, 71, 72, 88
Cambridge, college at, 136
Camelot, xii, 44, 143, 167, 169
Canterbury, 93
Canterbury, Archbishop of, 13
Catherine, 42, 83–9, 92, 98–9, 104, 164
Cauchon, Pierre, 108–9, 112, 115–17
Caxton, William, xi, xii, 173–4, 178–9
Cervantes, xi
Charles VI, 41–2, 45, 57–9, 73, 75, 83–4, 89, 98, 101, 104, 153, 176
Charles VII, 106, 111, 133, 146
Chaucer, Geoffrey, 74, 128
Chetwynd, John, 43
Chetwynd, Philip, 29–30, 43, 92, 107, 136, 139; as boy, 5, 6, 130; as page, 11, 21–2, 31, 42
Chinon, 105
Christmas, 14, 46, 81, 133–4
Churchill, Winston, 164, 168
Clarence, Duke of, 76–7, 88
Cobham, Eleanor, 132
Colchester, Malory at, 152
Coleshill, 134, 147, 151
Columbus, Christopher, xi
Common Market, 165
Compiègne, 108
Constance, 49, 50, 76
Coombe Abbey, 6, 147–8, 151, 175
Cornwall, 149–50

Cosne, siege of, 89–91
Coventry, xii, 6, 134, 152
Crécy, 10, 12, 27–8, 65–6

Dauphin, 57, 73, 83, 88–9, 101, 103, 105–6, 153; *see also* Charles VII
"Death Song of the British Kings," 5, 131
de Bordin, John, 57–8, 60
de Lisle family, 24, 39
Despencer, Isabella, 101
Discarded Image, The, 169
Domrémy, 104–5, 109, 113
Donatus, 7
Dorset, xii, 142, 148–9
Dover, 45–6, 85, 88, 93
Dugdale, William, 176

Edward the Confessor, 93
Edward, Prince of Wales, 152–3, 155, 157–8, 163–4
Edward I, and Arthur, 145
Edward III, 10, 27–9, 41, 48, 54, 57
Edward IV, 70–1, 154–8, 164, 166
Edward V, 164
Elaine, *see* Astolat
Eleanor, Queen, and Arthur, 145
Elizabeth, of York, 164
English, *vs* French, 10, 27–8, 41–7, 50–65, 73, 75–84, 88–90, 103, 131, 133, 136, 143, 146, 154, 164–5, 175; heir to crowns of, 101; and Joan of Arc, 104–5, 108, 118, 122
Eton, school at, 136
Exeter, Duke of, 91

Flanders, 20, 42, 55
French *vs* English, *see* English *vs* French
Froissart, Jean, 27, 57

Gaheret, *see* Gareth
Gaheris, and Guinevere, 120–1
Galahad, 39, 96, 102, 123, 131, 138–9, 143, 155–6, 168, 176
Gareth, 8, 15–17, 48, 96, 120–1, 130, 143, 168, 175
Gaucourt, Sire de, 51
Gawain, 96, 120, 168

INDEX

Geoffrey of Monmouth, 44, 142
Glastonbury, 95, 141, 145, 174, 178
Gloucester, Duke of, 91, 103, 132–3, 140–1, 164
"Goodman of Paris," 125–7
Greyfriars, xii, 4, 15, 26, 38, 74, 96, 159, 177–8
Guenièvre, *see* Guinevere
Guillaume, Brother, 7–9, 15
Guines, 46–8, 71
Guinevere, 8, 31, 33, 97–8, 120–1, 137–8, 141, 144–5, 168
Gutenberg, 179
Guy of Warwick, 33, 87, 102, 120
"Guy of Warwick," 22–4
Guy's Cliff, 23, 87–8, 102, 159
Gwayr, King, 20
Gwidard, King, 20

Hal, Prince, 11, 26, 29, 39
Harfleur, 39, 51–6, 70–1, 146, 175–6
Harley, Robert, 174
Harold the Saxon, 10
Hastings, 10
Henry IV, 8, 10–12, 26, 29, 39, 50
Henry V, xi, 43, 45, 48, 50, 55–9, 61–5, 71–3, 75, 83–8, 91, 107, 119, 152–3, 165, 170, 175–7; and Richard II, 39–40, 45, 50; coronation of, 40–1; illness and death of, 88–95, 101, 122; *see also* Beauchamp, Richard, *and* English *vs* French
Henry VI, 99, 102–4, 107–9, 120, 131–2, 136–7, 140–1, 149, 154–8, 164; knighting and crowning of, 103–4, 107, 111, 119–20; and shadows, 104, 123, 139, 152; and Margaret, 133, 137–8; in Tower, 153, 155
Henry VII, 164, 173
Holy Grail, 9, 16, 24, 26, 30, 94, 125, 131, 139, 141, 144–5, 167, 173
Holy Land, 9, 20, 26, 141
Holy Roman Empire, 49, 75
Hostell, Thomas, 70–1
Hundred Year's War, xii, 171
Huss, John, 49–50

Igraine, 141
Isabella, Countess, 25

Jacqueline of Hainaut, 103, 132
Joan of Arc, xii, 16, 31, 34, 104–6, 108–23, 136, 155, 165, 177
John the Fearless, *see* Burgundy, Duke of
John, King of France, 28, 42
Joseph of Arimathea, 139, 141–2
Jung, Carl, 171

Kay, Sir, 16
Kenilworth Castle, 43
Kent, 12–13, 148–9
Kirby Priory, 6

Lady of the Lake, 168
Lancastrians, xii, 70, 91, 99, 102, 139, 153–6, 158, 164, 166, 170; chart of, 160
Launcelot, xii–xiii, 8, 16, 26, 48, 78, 96, 123, 125, 127–8, 131, 143, 152, 155–6, 175–6; and Guinevere, 31, 33, 97–8, 121; and Urry, 34
Layamon, 142
Leicester, 103, 128
Lewis, C. S., xi, 167, 169–71
Lollards, 49
London, 13, 93, 132, 154–5, 158; Malory and, xii, 134, 137, 146, 150–1, 174–5; celebration in, 72–3, 84–5; terror in, 149
Louis XI, 154–7
Louvre, 84, 89
Lucan, 67
Ludgate, Malory at, 152
Luxemburg, John of, 108, 111
Lyonesse, Lady, 16
Lyonesse, 150
Lyonet, Lady, 16, 130

Maine, 138–41, 148
Maisoncelles, 60, 62, 64–5, 67, 177
Malory, Elizabeth, 32–3, 70, 128–30, 133–4, 143, 146, 159
Malory, John, 5–7, 9–12, 14, 41, 43, 76, 86, 103, 107, 131
Malory, Nicholas, xii, 32
Malory Robert, 32, 134, 143, 156
Malory, Thomas, 96, 101–2, 107–9, 123, 125, 132–4, 136, 141–3, 159, 164; known and guessed facts about, xi–

193

INDEX

Malory, Thomas (*continued*)
xiii, 165–71, 174–7, 179; and Henry V, xi, 55, 72–3, 86, 92, 95, 170; and Joan of Arc, xii, 34, 110, 113–17, 120–2, 155, 177; in prison, xii, 3, 4, 14, 15, 30–1, 34–5, 37–9, 44–5, 48, 55, 65, 69–71, 74, 104, 127, 130, 145, 152, 157, 165, 167, 179; charges against, xii, 38, 151–2; as a boy, 3–15, 130; mother of, 6, 14–15, 86; as page, 11, 19, 21–2, 24, 27, 31, 40–2; training of, for knighthood, 13–14, 27, 29–30; and French wars, 43–5, 51, 53, 54, 57–8, 61–7, 71–3, 77–9, 81, 88–90, 176–7; knighting of, 78; and Catherine, 85–6, 98–9; and women, 96–8, 127–8; and Henry VI, 103–4, 120, 155, 156; and Henry Beauchamp, 130, 131, 138–9; pilgrimage of, 142–6, 149–50; and new fellowship, 147–8, 151–2; and Edward IV, 154, 158, 163; grave of, 163, 178; father of, *see* Malory, John; *see also* Greyfriars, *Morte Darthur*, Newbold Revel, *and under items throughout*

Margaret of Anjou, 133, 137–8, 140–1, 148–9, 152–3, 155–8, 164
Marne River, 88
Marshalsea Prison, 152
Martin V, Pope, 76
Master of Game, The, 86
Meaux, siege of, 88–9
Merlin, 5, 96, 105, 125, 142, 144, 168, 174
Monks Kirby, xi, 6–7, 15, 136, 141, 147–8, 159, 175
Montereau, 83, 106
Mordred, 44, 65–6, 96, 143, 154, 168
More, Thomas, xi
Morgan Library, 174, 178
Mort Artu, 136
Morte Arthur, Le, 66–7, 94
Morte Arthure, 175
Morte Darthur, xi–xiii, 8–9, 15–17, 24, 26, 31–5, 38–9, 44, 48, 55–6, 65–7, 94–7, 102, 121, 123, 125, 127–8, 137, 139, 142, 145–6, 156, 158, 165–9, 173–80
Mountford, Baldwin, 147
Mountford, William, 134, 151

Neville, Anne Beauchamp, 38–9, 131
Neville, Anne, 157
Neville, Cecily, 131
Neville, Richard, 153–4, 156–8, 163; wife of, 38–9, 131; and Malory, 38, 67, 134–5, 142, 154, 156, 158–9
Newbold Revel, xii, 4, 8, 12, 14, 32, 41, 43, 76, 86–7, 133, 139, 146–7, 151, 154, 175
Newgate, 37, 69, 74, 98, 134, 177; Malory in, *see* Malory, in prison
Noble Tale of King Arthur and the Emperor Lucius, The, 55–6
Normandy, 41, 76, 78, 84, 90
Northampton, 153
Northumberland, 154
Notre Dame Cathedral, 84, 119
Nuneaton, 151
"Nut Brown Maid, The," 129

Oakeshott, Walter, xii–xiii
Orléans, Joan in, 105
Orléans, Duke of, 42, 59, 71, 73–5, 132
Oxford, 44, 132
Owein, 5

Page, John, 79–82
Paris, 73, 78, 84–5, 88–9, 106–7, 119, 132
Parliament, 102, 107, 146, 148, 149, 158; Malory and, 113, 133–6, 140, 142, 148
Parsival, 24
Paston, John, 166
Pepys, P. A. L., 175
Philip, Duke of Burgundy, 83; *see also* Burgundy, Duke of
Picardy, 51
Poitiers, 10, 12, 28, 41–2, 65–6
Pontoise, prisoners at, 133
Portsmouth, Henry V and, 50

Raleigh, Walter, xi
Revel, Hervis de, 32
Rheims, 105–6, 119
Richard II, 12–13, 39–40, 45, 50
Richard III, 164
Robin Hood, 130
Rouen, xii, 16, 31, 34, 78–9, 107–19, 128, 136, 146, 155, 165, 177; siege and

INDEX

surrender of, 79–82; king's casket at, 93; dungeon of castle at, 114
Round Table, see Arthur, names of knights, and Winchester
Rous, John, 141–2, 159

St. Albans, 153
St. Bartholomew's, 4
St. Crispin and St. Crispinian, 61
St. Denis, king's casket at, 93
St. Edith's, 7, 11–12, 129, 175
St. Edward, 95, 174
St. Francis, chapel of, 163
St. George, heart of, 48, 75
St. Martin's, 55
St. Mary's, 122–3, 141
St. Nicholas, Calais, 107
St. Nicholas, London, 4
St. Ouen's, 115
St. Paul, xi
St. Paul's, 4, 73, 174
St. Peter's, 78
Salisbury, 143–4
Salisbury, Earl of, 131
Seine River, 76, 78, 80, 83, 88, 94, 118, 131, 133
Shakespeare, William, 167, 175–6
Shambles, of London, 3, 134
Sigismund, 48–9, 75–6
Smyth, Hugh, 32, 151–2
Smyth, Joan, 151–2
Somme River, 57–9
Southampton, 44–5, 137
Stafford, Earl of, 111, 136
Stafford, Humphrey, see Buckingham, Duke of
Stonehenge, 144
Stormfield, 128–9
Suffolk, Earl of, 65, 105, 132, 140–1, 148; and wife for Henry VI, 133, 138; death of, 148–9
"Summer is a-coming in," 5

Ternoise River, 60
Tewkesbury, 131, 139, 163–4
Thoreau, Henry, 165
Tichfield Abbey, 138
Tintagel, 150, 174
Tower of London, and guns, 43; prisoners in, 73; Malory in, 152; Henry VI and Margaret in, 153, 155, 164
Trinity Royal, 50
Tristan, *see* Tristram
Tristram, xii–xiii, 8, 32, 38, 86, 96, 121, 125
Troyes, 83–4
Tudor, Henry, *see* Henry VII
Tudor, Owen, 98, 164
Tyler, Wat, 13, 106

Urry, 34
Uther, King, xii

"Victory Song of Agincourt," 73
Vinaver, Eugène, 167, 175

Wace, Robert, 142
Wakefield, 153
Wareham, 148–9
Wars of the Roses, xii, 153–6, 163–6, 170–1
Warwick, Earl of, *see* Beauchamp, Richard, *and* Neville, Richard
Warwick, earls of, 9, 20, 40, 47, 141
Warwick Castle, 3–4, 12, 20–1, 134; Malory and, 11, 19, 21–4, 27, 29–30, 40–3, 87, 130, 136, 159; dungeon of, 31, 114, 175; royal visit to, 86–7
Warwickshire, xi, xii, 6, 8, 41, 51, 76, 107, 133, 136, 158, 163
Westminster Abbey, 39–40, 84–5, 95, 98–9, 103–4, 138, 174
Whittington, Richard, 4
William the Conqueror, 10, 41, 77, 120
Wiltshire, xii, 140, 142–3
Winchester, 42, 44, 164; manuscript at, xii–xiii; Round Table at, 44, 143, 170, 174, 178
Winchester, Bishop of, 91
Windsor, 84, 88–9
Woodville, Elizabeth, 157
Wycliffe, John, 49

York, Edward, Duke of, 65, 86–7
York, Richard, Duke of, 140, 152–4
Yorkists, xii, 32, 70, 140, 152–6, 163–4, 170; chart of, 161

195